Ann Girdharry was born and educated in the UK. A trained psychotherapist, she worked for many years as a manager in the not-for-profit sector. Today, she lives in Montpellier, France with her husband and two children.

You can find out more about Ann Girdharry by visiting her website – www.girdharry.com

Or catch up with her on social media –

www.goodreads.com/AnnGirdharry
www.bookbub.com/profile/ann-girdharry
www.facebook.com/AnnGirdharryAuthor/

Titles by this author

Kal Medi series

Good Girl Bad Girl
London Noir
The Beauty Killers

Chilling Tales of the Unexpected
Boxed Set

The Beauty Killers

Ann Girdharry

For Christophe

xxx

Chapter One

The walls are covered with photographs.

All our guests, past and present, stare back at me from rows of coloured, glossy squares. I like being surrounded by their beauty.

We have four guest rooms. At the moment, two of our rooms are empty, and it's my job to put that right.

Let me tell you about the last guest who checked out – she was blonde and she had lovely, long, glossy hair. Her performance on our catwalk was one of my favourites. Unfortunately, my Brother didn't feel the same way and he has more say in things than I do.

I work as the scout.

I'd picked that blonde out after weeks, no maybe months, of searching. Once she'd been selected, we lured her in. Then we kept her in one of our guest rooms. In the end her hair began falling out in handfuls. It was such a shame and she became so ugly the decision was made to get rid of her. What a pity after all those years of enjoyment.

Since her exit, our remaining two guests are behaving impeccably – so that's a bonus.

Anyway, I've been told to vary the game plan. Again we want a blonde and this time we want a specimen with more staying power. I've been scouting, and here's the good news –

I've spotted a possible. Let's see what the others have to say about her. I think they'll be pleased.

Chapter Two

Detective Chief Inspector Spinks sat on the park bench in front of the lake. It was his usual place to meet Kal, in St James Park right in the centre of London. His grey suit appeared immaculate against the shabby slats of the bench. Spinks caught a waft of cut grass as the gardener drove past on his motorised mower.

Kal always arrived on time and, for once, Spinks arrived early – to settle his nerves perhaps. He touched the gold eagle pin at his lapel, running his fingers over the pointed edges of its wings.

Spinks didn't need to close his eyes to see the face of Ivana's mother. He saw Mrs Stanislova's face in his nightmares. Her accusing eyes seemed to follow him through the day as time dragged on since her daughter's disappearance.

He shifted on the bench. He'd soon make Kal a very dangerous proposal and one he knew she'd find hard to resist. Spinks rubbed his hands together and was upset to find them sweaty. He was over-thinking this one. Kal was perfect for the job. In fact, she was brilliant and she didn't even know it. That young woman was one of a kind. So why was he nervous? Because he didn't want to lose a second young woman to the same killer? Or because this case involved a personal risk as well as a professional one? Spinks stared out at the water of the lake. London could seem so bleak at this time of year with frosty mornings and dreary skies and the lake was a cold sheet of silver. He had no choice – Kal was his best chance. And in his heart of hearts, he knew she was likely his last hope.

Kal approached, walking at a brisk pace and watching Detective Chief Inspector Spinks from afar. DCI Spinks would only contact her for something important, and very likely, something involving life and death and the inner workings of the criminal mind. Yes, she was an expert on criminality. It made her an asset in Spink's war against London's underworld.

As she sat beside him, Kal noticed the white hairs at his temple. Almost twenty years her senior, Spinks looked as if he'd aged overnight, though she'd only seen him recently. A top man in the police force, today he looked greyer than usual, as if ingrained with the grime of London.

'Spring will soon be here and I shall be glad to see it,' Spinks said. 'Do you remember how we first met at this time of year?'

Yes, Kal remembered. So much had happened between them since then. At the beginning, she hadn't liked him and hadn't trusted him. So much had changed.

'Oh no. I hope you didn't invite me all the way here to talk about the weather.'

Spinks smiled. With long, black hair and a dark complexion, Kal gazed at him with a fierce intensity. He was sure most people would find it difficult to meet her eye. She had the same cool exterior and the same lack of social graces as that first time they met. Underneath all the front, he now knew Kal as an expert in psychology. A woman with a mind capable of matching the most devious of criminals. After all, she'd been trained by a master – her father – and she'd already proved herself a match for some of the most twisted minds Spinks had encountered.

He cleared his throat. 'Detective Sergeant Jennifer Morris has been missing for two days. She's one of my best operatives.'

He passed over a paper and Kal stared at an attractive woman, late twenties, with her blonde hair pulled up into a neat chignon for her police officer shot. Officer Morris had a serious yet open face, the type, Kal thought, who would generate a lot of trust from colleagues and from the public.

She made to hand back the photograph.

'Keep it.'

Kal frowned. Her father's training in analysing people had been demanding. That's what made her so good at what she did and she'd not seen Spinks like this before. He was agitated and ill at ease. Organised crime was Spink's speciality. He knew the score – high risk investigations that put him in line for violence if things went wrong, sick killers who didn't give a damn and would take a life in the blink of an eye. What was different today? She scrutinised him and couldn't put her finger it. Beyond the obvious of course, which was he believed officer Morris might already be dead.

'What's the story?' she asked.

'Over a stretch of years, five bodies have turned up in south west London. All young women. All with cutting of their wrist arteries and blood loss was the cause of death. Though no blood was present at the scene and the bodies had been drained. None of the victims have been identified. Within the same target area, two other women have been reported missing in the last two years. The only useful intelligence I've got is one of them used a day centre for street sleepers. It was a hunch, but I felt pretty certain the murdered women must have been street sleepers and that was why they'd never been identified. I set up an operation and sent Detective Sergeant Morris in undercover. She was working as a volunteer at the day centre.'

Spinks handed Kal two more photographs.

'These are the two other missing women – Ivana and Ruth.'

'Anything else linking the recent disappearances with the bloodless corpses?'

'Nothing. But my experience tells me we're on the right track.'

Kal nodded.

'All five victims were malnourished. The coroner found syringe marks on one of them, though no trace of drugs. You know as well as I do there aren't many ways five young women go missing and have no family or friends searching for them. It makes the itinerant community a very likely source. As to who's behind it and the motivation – we've drawn a complete blank.'

'Officer Morris must have been on to something.'

'It doesn't add up. Right up until the day she disappeared, she hadn't found anything of substance. In fact, I was about to call the whole thing off.'

He'd certainly got her attention.

Spinks cleared his throat. 'And no new… bodies have been recovered.'

Most people would have missed the micro-hesitation before that word. Yes, she thought, though he hid it well, Spinks couldn't stop thinking about officer Jennifer Morris turning up dead, most likely with the same cutting as the other women and the same bloodless body.

'What do you think?' Spinks asked.

His hand was drifting towards a gold eagle pin at his lapel.

Given everything he'd told her, what Kal thought was Jennifer Morris' body would turn up soon. After that, there would be another victim, and then another and on and on, until someone cracked the sick mind behind this and found out the who, the how and the why. The itinerant community was an easy target and she didn't like that at all. And the person to crack this case, she thought with satisfaction, would be her.

'I'll do it,' she said. 'It takes a criminal to catch a criminal, right?'

'You're not a criminal Kal, and we both know that.'

'So why me?'

'Because you're the best I've got.'

The direct statement took her by surprise.

She laughed to hide her embarrassment. 'Yeah, and I think like a criminal and my murdering father took so many lives I can work my ass off for the rest of my life to make up for it, and I'll still not balance the scales.'

She didn't call the way her father trained her "brainwashing" any more, not since she realised she could use it for the good, and when she did, it dissolved a bit of the sickness she felt about her own bloodline. That didn't stop every day feeling like she dragged a dead weight behind her. But each time she helped someone in dire need, it hacked away a bit of the burden. Meeting Spinks that first time had saved her.

'Let's get to work,' she said.

They understood each other. Kal had the skills, the guts and the strategies to slip amongst the bad guys like a shadow.

She took one more glance at Jennifer Morris. Then she waited, because she could see Spinks had something else he wanted to say.

Spinks was staring at the silvery water of the lake. A couple of ducks were paddling across its icy-looking surface. Spinks was a tall and hawk-nosed man, and when he finally spoke, his voice came out surprisingly soft.

'This is a bad one, Kal. I'm sorry to ask, only I can't risk another officer.'

'I know that. You don't need to explain.'

Strange again. As far as Kal was concerned, she'd left Detective Chief Inspector Spinks with an open invitation to use her skills and she stood by that promise.

'Like I said, I'll do it, and you know how I love a challenge.'

Spinks met her gaze. 'I'll say it again, you're a very unusual young woman.'

Kal laughed. 'Sure I know, and I think you and I make a great team. Don't worry, if officer Morris was on to something, I'll find out. And if she's still alive, I'll do my very best to find her.'

Chapter Three

Jennifer Morris lay in the pitch black.

She had a stabbing pain in her head and her wrist was throbbing. She couldn't remember anything. In fact, she couldn't think of much at all, not even who she was. Her head was fogged up and thoughts kept slipping away. It was like one hell of a bad hangover and much more besides.

The floor was smooth and smelled musty. Groaning, she rolled to the side and gave a gasp as her wrist scraped the ground.

'For God's sake shut up!'

The whisper was full of fear. It sounded so urgent she stopped breathing. The hair at the back of her neck stood on end.

After a few seconds, slowly and carefully, she pushed onto her knees. Her heart hammered and she waited, hoping it would calm. Staring out into the dark, she couldn't make out a single thing. Should she answer? Should she curl up and hope the other person went away? She couldn't think what would be best to do. In the end, she couldn't stand it any longer.

She did her best to make her voice steady. 'Who's there?'

'Shut up. Don't make a noise or they'll come for you.'

This was crazy. It didn't make any sense. She shook her head but her thoughts wouldn't come into line. The voice was a woman's and it came from nearby though not really close.

On her knees, she inched her way in the direction of the voice. She was stopped by something cold and hard. Reaching out her good hand she felt vertical metal bars. Prison bars, said a thought in her head, and that idea made her heart hammer even faster.

Everything was so pitch black. Why the hell were there no lights?

And she couldn't stand the silence.

'Who are you?' she said.

A second voice spoke, again from the other side of the bars, except this time from the left.

'Are you stupid or something!' the voice hissed. 'You want to be dead? Shut the fuck up.'

Now her heart thumped like it might burst.

The first voice spoke again in the same urgent whisper. 'You're new and you'll get to understand. Stay quiet and do as you're told, then they'll leave you alone. And for fuck's sake don't cry. You've got to make like you're happy.'

Her head began spinning.

Part of her wanted to laugh and another part wanted to vomit. This was real. This was terror – she could hear it in the women's voices. No, more than hearing it, she could *feel* it. She could feel their terror in her bones.

Her whole body started shaking. Don't be frightened, she told herself, this can't be real. This was a nightmare. It was all wrong and soon she'd wake up and everything would be all right. Pushing her head against the metal, she tried to make herself wake up.

The more she ground her head against the bars, the more their warnings rang in her ears. She pressed her eyes shut and tried not to scream.

Chapter Four

'Kal are you crazy!' Marty said. 'Oh no, don't say anything because I already know the answer.'

Marty threw herself onto Kal's sofa. 'When I said we'd be partners in combatting crime I didn't mean partners *in death*.'

'Calm down,' Kal said. 'We agreed we'd work the next case together. You even begged me for it. Make your damn mind up.'

Kal stalked into the kitchen and began banging cupboard doors and then mugs down onto the counter top. She shouted in the direction of the lounge.

'In this game, you can't be half in. You've got to be all in or not at all.'

She'd known Marty since they were children, both joining the same primary school and both seen as the two misfit, new girls who'd be outsiders forever. Teaming up then had been natural.

It had worked even better when the two of them joined the same kung fu class. They'd gone on to train together for years. Both of them had been competitive and Kal was proud to say Marty had won the National Championship more than once.

Marty was her best friend, well, Kal had to admit, maybe her only friend.

The kettle clicked off and she rummaged in the cupboard for tea bags.

They'd already worked on two tough cases together, though this would be the first they didn't fall into by accident. She carried two full mugs from the kitchen. Kal couldn't risk being anything but harsh because Marty had to understand the rules of survival.

She put the drinks down. 'Do you want it or don't you?'

'I told you I did and I meant it. It's just... oh I don't know, I don't feel comfortable with the plan.'

'Which bit don't you like?'

'How about any of it.'

Kal sprayed out a mouthful of tea as she laughed.

'Now you're exaggerating. All you need to do is set up a health education programme. You're such a health freak it'll be a piece of cake getting all those experts to come and do sessions and talks. Clarence House has even got its own exercise studio so in between you can probably spend hours doing exactly what you like doing most – punishing yourself in the gym – so what's to argue about?'

'First of all, I'm not a health freak, I take my life habits seriously that's all. Unlike some of us.'

Marty waggled a finger in Kal's direction.

'Secondly, that's not what I'm talking about and you know it. I'm okay working at the day centre. The bit I don't like is you spinning off on your own. Spinks has five women who were bled out or drained or some other shit, and then their bodies were dumped. The only information we've got is the autopsy report of death by exsanguination and the coroner's speculation of some kind of ritual sacrifice. Then officer Morris goes missing and you're planning on going it alone on the streets, cool as a cucumber, hoping some psycho crawls out of the woodwork? That's not a plan, that's insane.'

'Whoever's taking young women, they're the insane ones. And if you've got a better idea, spit it out. No, we need to go in and we've got to flush them out.'

Kal took a second sip of her peppermint tea.

'The day centre, Clarence House, is a good lead, and that's your domain, Marty. I'll be covering the street network. I don't see where there's a problem.'

Marty had leadership skills and she had people skills. She also had technology expertise from her work in security management. In fact, Marty had recently given up a top job so she could work with Kal. As far as Kal was concerned, she'd make an excellent spy in the camp.

She waited for Marty's answer.

Kal had already decided they wouldn't go in under Jennifer's cover story. It was too tame, not to mention blown. No, Marty would take the centre, while she went in at grassroots level. It would mean sleeping rough because the people with the real intelligence would be the homeless community and she needed to get close to them. She'd give Marty the far safer option.

Blowing steam from her drink, she sat back on the sofa. A few months ago, to flush out a psychopath, she'd posed as a prostitute. This was her next challenge. She watched over the top of her mug as Marty battled her doubts.

It was ironic to see Marty struggling. Ironic because Kal knew it was Marty who kept her on the straight path. Marty's good influence had always kept her the right side of the line. Marty with her strong moral compass and unshakeable ethics. It had been like that since the first day they met. Marty was the one dragging Kal out of arguments and fights and smoothing things over. She'd done it all the way through their childhood and adolescence. Did Marty know how important she was? How she kept Kal tied down to some semblance of a normal life? No, she likely had no idea, because Kal never told her.

Marty studied the picture of Jennifer Morris. She'd already examined the shots of the other young women. The dead ones.

Going over to the window, Marty looked down over Wimbledon common where a man walked along with his dog. Nearby, a woman waited at a bus stop. They were ordinary people going about their ordinary business, except sometimes, for some people, something nasty came along. Especially when you were at the bottom of the pile like those homeless girls.

Marty shivered. The last two cases she'd worked with Kal had changed her. Something had shifted in Marty ever since she'd been left for dead in an alley. Then she'd fought for the life of a young boy, and after being stuck in a cellar with him dying beside her, something inside had shifted so far it would never go back. She knew she could never return to her old life.

Marty turned to face her friend. Leaning against the cushions, Kal had a look on her face Marty couldn't read. That must be a look Kal used when she was working – one that was meant to throw people off the trail. She probably learned it from her nasty father. Yes, thought Marty, if anyone could find Jennifer Morris before it was too late, it was Kal.

'Like I explained, your job will be to get close to people at the day centre and get them talking to you,' Kal said. 'According to Spinks, the staff are really shaken about Jennifer going missing. It's an excellent time to go in and find out everything you can about those people.'

'You make it sound simple.'

'That's because it is. Intelligence gathering is about collecting all the little details and when the picture comes together, it's what's missing or is out of place that points the way forward. Your aim is to get in close. You're good at that because people like you. It's your strength.'

'They'd like you too, except you're always glaring and scaring people off.'

'Exactly.'

Kal knew she came across badly, so no point in whining about it. Best to simply get on with what she was better at.

Marty made her decision. She would trust Kal with her life and, more importantly, she knew Kal needed her. Needed her to tame down the part of Kal that was too reckless. The part that was too much of a loner. The part of Kal that took too many risks. She would work with the staff at Clarence House and when she did, she'd be there to watch Kal's back.

'Okay, count me in,' she said.

Chapter Five

Mrs Stanislova worked as an office cleaner. The pay was bad and the hours long and unsocial. On the upside, it was steady work, which meant she could pull together the rent for her one-bed flat.

She didn't care about the run-down neighbourhood, she didn't care she had to budget every penny, she didn't care if the neighbours were noisy and the buses ran inches away from her windows and there was mould on the bathroom walls and no hot water. All she cared about was finding her daughter. That's why she'd come to London.

She'd given up her life to search for Ivana. To everything she held sacred, Mrs Stanislova had sworn she wouldn't leave this country without her daughter. She would see this through to the end, even if it meant being buried here, alone, in this foreign land.

On the other side of the road, Kal waited. A stray dog nosed around some bins, a toddler cried in one of the high-rise blocks but no normal people were walking the streets. It wasn't wise to be out and about in this part of town, not unless you were part of a group and had the safety of numbers. This was a dangerous area with plenty of knife attacks.

At the end of the street, she clocked two young men hanging around. They were clearly gang members and this was their turf. Rather than waiting for them to come to her, she decided to pass the time with a small chat. She was sure they'd appreciate it.

As Kal wandered over, they eyed her up. With jeans slung low, they showed half their underwear. The two of them had perfected the habit of being able to slouch and flex their chest and show off their muscles at the same time – a combination Kal was astonished anyone could master. They were two local thugs confident of their status. Confident it was two against one and that she was a woman walking into danger. She was sure they anticipated easy prey.

'Hello guys.'

One of them snorted. The other let his eyelids droop.

'Whatcha doin' round here, babe? You lookin' for a good time?'

These two were certainly into drugs and the odd stabbing of a rival. They'd grown up on violence.

Now she was up close, Kal saw how they got a little nervous. She'd put a killer, dead look on her face – the same one her father used to quell his victims and make them shit their pants. The one that said there were no limits. Stature and size didn't matter because the intent said it all.

She watched as they realised they'd badly misjudged her, except pride and gang mentality wouldn't allow them to back down. She didn't want to get into a fight. What she wanted was for them to piss the hell off from Mrs Stanislova's street.

Kal flexed her fingers. She wasn't an expert in Dim-mak for nothing – Dim-mak was the ancient art of using pressure points to inflict serious injury. Once, her father had fought her almost to the death with it. He'd said it was an essential lesson.

'I'm not looking for trouble,' she said. 'Thing is, a friend of mine lives around here and I'd like to make sure this street stays clean. Know what I mean?'

They were sizing her up properly now. Trying to decide if she was worth the trouble. Part of her hoped they'd decide to go for it, but that was the reckless part, the bit that always got her into messes she'd have been wiser to keep out of.

One of them nodded slowly. People could feel that edge in someone. They could sense blood violence. Know when the person in front of them was capable of snapping like a twig. And Kal knew how to turn all of that on, thanks to her father, David Khan.

'Great. Because if I hear anything has happened to her, I'll know who to come looking for, won't I?'

Taking another step forward, she let her whole body prepare, ready for any retaliation. Of course, they'd carry weapons, but she didn't think they'd use them today.

One of them started to gently back off, all the while making it look like he wasn't. Trying not to lose face, they slouched and mooched and took their time at it, their baggy pants swinging almost around their knees.

'Yeah, no problem gorgeous, I get yer.'

'Stay cool babe.'

'See you around then,' she said.

Kal laughed inwardly. People sure as hell didn't warm to her nor like her, but she could make them respect her when it mattered, and in this line of work, that counted for a lot.

It wasn't long before Mrs Stanislova appeared and began struggling up the steps with a bag full of groceries. She looked much older than the forty-five years it stated on Spinks' report.

The woman hadn't even glanced around as she'd pulled out her keys. Either she had nothing to steal or she didn't put much of a price on her own life. Or both. Kal shoved her hands in her pockets. For over a year this woman had been pounding on Spinks' door for news of her daughter. Kal knew she must be careful not to raise Mrs Stanislova's hopes because that would be cruelty in the extreme.

'Excuse me, are you Mrs Stanislova?'

The keys fell with a clatter. As Mrs Stanislova turned, Kal caught the flash of hope in her eyes. Of course, any stranger could be someone with information about her daughter – any stranger, any phone call, any letter or email. Kal took a deep breath and then breathed out long and slow. It helped her push her own feelings aside and remain focused. The poor woman was living a life of torture.

Bending to pick up the keys, Kal gave a small smile.

'I wondered if we could have a talk about your daughter, Ivana?' She carried on quickly. 'I'm sorry I don't have any news and I know she's been missing for over a year. I wanted to find out a little more about her.'

The woman was shorter than Kal and she squinted as she peered up.

'I don't understand, who are you? You're not a reporter because none of the damn newspapers are interested in a nobodies like me. And from the looks of you you're not police.'

The woman had an accent and she had an edge of wariness born of bad experiences. It must have been so hard living here on her own. Spinks told Kal that Ivana's mother arrived in London three months after last hearing from her daughter. It had taken her that long to borrow, beg and scrape together enough money to travel over from Poland. Since then, Mrs Stanislova went to see Spinks every two weeks, and, to his credit, he never turned her away. Though the trail had long since grown cold and the more time passed the less likely were the chances of finding any missing person.

'Please, could we talk inside? I won't take much of your time.'

The woman leaned closer. 'Did you know Ivana?'

There was an eagerness in her voice.

'I'm sorry, I didn't know your daughter, Mrs Stanislova. I'm here because I want to help find her or find out what happened to her. Please can we talk inside?'

A bus rumbled past, blowing out a plume of fumes. They both stopped talking and waited until the noise died down.

Looking Kal up and down, Mrs Stanislova curled her lip. 'A slip of a girl like you? What the hell do you think you can do? And why would you? I've no money to give. Why are you here, did you see the missing persons piece they did in the "Big Issue"?'

The Big Issue – the magazine produced for and by the homeless community and widely distributed on the streets of the capital. That would be her way in.

'Yes, I did. I've slept rough myself and now I help loved ones when someone goes missing. Besides, don't be fooled by appearances, Mrs Stanislova. Finding the truth has more to do with strategy than it does with how someone looks. At least, that's what I've found to be true.'

'You talk cute and that doesn't mean a thing.'

'Oh but it does, because we both know Ivana went places the law doesn't go. Now do you want my help finding what happened to your daughter or don't you?'

Ivana's mother crumpled and Kal felt a twinge of regret for having to push so hard to get inside the door.

'Let me help you with that,' she said.

The woman nodded, her resistance suddenly evaporated. What was left was an exhausted shell of a mother who clearly understood more about her daughter than she'd wanted to tell the police. Kal gently took the shopping and followed Mrs Stanislova inside.

***

Making a hot drink for a guest is a ritual which sets the tone for a polite meeting and people cling to those rituals, especially in times of distress. Kal waited, listening as cups and saucers were arranged on a tray and carried, rattling, into the main room. Fumes from the street seemed to have seeped their way inside and Kal tried not to stare at the grey-stained net curtains and the shabby furniture.

Mrs Stanislova had regained her composure and she sat down in an arm chair. Kal was already perched on a grubby sofa which smelled strongly of coffee stains.

'Detective Chief Inspector Spinks has been kind. I know he feels sorry for me.' Mrs Stanislova shook her head. 'The Big Issue have been the only ones who've offered any help. Their monthly missing persons feature is a godsend.'

She had to tread carefully and not say anything that might later lead back to her and threaten her cover story. Still, Kal felt she wanted to give something.

'All I can say is I'm a friend and I'm not here for profit. I don't want your money, I don't want anything except to find the truth.'

'Did you have a bad experience yourself? Did you run away from home?'

'Something like that and I intend to use all my knowledge and skills to get to the bottom of these disappearances. I can't explain why, it's something... personal.'

Which was exactly the truth. It *was* personal, because Kal felt deep inside the need to atone for her father's crimes.

Mrs Stanislova must have heard the ring of truth in it because she seemed to accept the explanation.

'Could you tell me about Ivana, please? And what you know of the time leading up to her disappearance.'

Kal had absorbed the details from the police files but hearing it directly could always give clues and ideas that would never come from reading it on a page. Besides, she'd come here for two reasons – to find out first-hand about Ivana and also to discover more about what it was that had got to Spinks.

Kal knew him to be a shrewd and skilled detective, able to work professionally under great pressure. A man whose experience was vital and precious and much needed on active cases. So what was it about Mrs Stanislova that made Spinks sweat? Why had he allowed this woman to have access to him on a regular basis, long after it was necessary? What was it about this woman that haunted him?

Mrs Stanislova reached behind to a dresser. There came a squeak of wood against wood as a drawer was pulled open.

'These are photographs and all her letters.'

Mrs Stanislova's hands were shaking as she passed over the bundle.

'It was my brother who paid for Ivana to come to London. Ivana wrote home every month without fail. We don't have internet connection at home and she knew I'd be reading her letter out to the whole family.'

'Your daughter's very attractive,' Kal said.

'I know, thank you. And she only sent us good news in her letters and told us about all her funny little discoveries here. There was never any sign things weren't going to plan. She was optimistic.'

Kal leafed through photographs of a good-looking blonde family. All the girls were pretty and Ivana stood out as beautiful, even when she was a small child. In the pictures, Kal could see Ivana got her looks from her mother and it was shocking how Mrs Stanislova's own beauty had been washed out by the months of agony and not-knowing – Kal hardly recognised the woman sitting in front of her. She could imagine the mother's strength dissolving little by little, as she clung on to the melting hope of finding her daughter.

'You see Ivana wanted to be an actress from when she was tiny. It was all she dreamed of. That's why my brother paid for her to come here.'

So many young girls came to London with the same dream. And for many of them, things did not turn out well.

'Acting is a very difficult profession to break in to,' Kal said.

'That's the thing. Ivana told us she'd made contact with an agent. She was already getting small jobs and she was hopeful for a big break. She told us she was getting close.'

Kal groaned inwardly. Of course, Ivana told her family the news they wanted to hear – that she was finding her way. Making it in the big city. That her lucky break was just around the corner. Kal could imagine the family readings of Ivana's letters and the gasps of admiration from her siblings and the pride of her parents. Goodness knows what Ivana had really gotten in to.

'Did she talk about friends?'

'She'd met another girl, called Megan and I don't know where she was from except I know she wasn't Polish. I've been trying to find Megan and yes, I know that sounds silly but I ask everywhere I go and I show pictures of Ivana. I spend my time at bus stops and train stations and handing out flyers on the underground. I've printed hundreds and hundreds of them where I do my cleaning jobs.'

Mrs Stanislova flapped one of them in Kal's face.

'If anyone ever finds out I'm using my employer's printers I'll get the sack. But I don't care. Sometimes I volunteer at a soup kitchen except no one has ever said they've seen Ivana.'

'It's a huge metropolis, Mrs Stanislova. The chances of meeting someone who knew your daughter are...'

'Zero? Oh yes, I know the statistics. What was your name again?'

'Kal.'

'Oh dear, I apologise. Sometimes I even forget what day it is. And as for being social, I'm sorry, I don't think I asked your name at the beginning did I? Anyway Kal, I know the figures and I can see you've no children of your own. If you've never been a mother there's no way you'll understand *this*.'

Mrs Stanislova placed her palm over her own chest. Kal stared at it.

'I *know* Ivana is alive. I know it inside. Of course, Mr Spinks has tried to warn me the chances of finding her are fading. Only I *know* she's out there. I know because if she would have died I'd have felt it. In here.'

Her hand was still pressed over her heart.

'Right.'

Kal cleared her throat. It wasn't her place to try to change how the woman felt. That would be disrespectful, not to mention pointless. It was obvious the belief in her daughter's survival was about all that was keeping this woman going.

It was also clear that a man like Spinks would take the lack of closure for Mrs Stanislova as a personal failure. Only she didn't think that was enough to explain why he couldn't let this woman go.

'As you say, I'm not a mother myself so I have to go on the situation as I see it. You said you're checking the underground and train stations, and I can understand that. But why are you checking the soup kitchen?'

'I'm not a fool, young lady. I know Ivana might have been putting a shine on things because she didn't want to disappoint us. Maybe things weren't going as well as she was making out.'

Mrs Stanislova fussed with a pile of magazines and newspapers. The one on the top was an old edition of the Big Issue.

'Ivana never asked for money and now I live here I see how expensive everything is. It's not like at home at all. But I want you to know Ivana was a good girl. I don't believe she'd be involved in anything against the law.'

Kal kept her thoughts to herself. In her view, likely Ivana had been tempted into something very unsavoury or illegal. So many young girls were duped into prostitution or fell prey to predators who used them as drug runners and such like. Desperation pushed them to it.

She reached out to take the cup of lukewarm coffee and stared at the murky surface. She had enough information from Mrs Stanislova to be pretty certain the mother wasn't implicated nor was she purposely covering something up.

Kal put her cup down and saw how it was interpreted, correctly, as her intention to leave. Mrs Stanislova couldn't hide the despair behind her eyes and Kal had to look away.

'I'm going to do my best, I promise,' she said, reaching out and taking Mrs Stanislova's hand. She was horrified to see a tear running down the woman's face.

'I can't stand it,' Mrs Stanislova whispered. 'Some days I'm sure I'm going mad. Or that I am already crazy.'

'Is there anything you didn't tell the police? Any tiny detail? Anything you've thought of since?'

Mrs Stanislova started to quietly cry. 'Nothing. There's nothing at all. I'd give my own life, I'd give anything, *anything*, for Ivana. Remember that Kal, my life for hers.'

Kal looked down at Mrs Stanislova's hand. It felt small between her own palms.

'How old was Ivana when she came to London?'

'She was seventeen.'

It had said that in the police file.

'Yes and I can see from the family shots she looked mature for her age.'

Mrs Stanislova nodded.

'She wasn't fazed to come to a new country all on her own?'

'Ivana spoke good English. She watched American movies constantly and she was very sensible. Of course, now I wish I'd sent her with one of her sisters. But the travel costs were high and we couldn't afford it for two and Ivana was the one with the best chances.'

'I see. Your brother, the one who funded Ivana coming over here, what does he have to say about it all?'

'My husband had a big fight with him. My husband said it was my brother's fault. That he'd put ideas into Ivana's head. Which wasn't true. It was Ivana herself who wanted to come. We don't talk to my brother anymore.'

Mrs Stanislova sounded hollow. The poor woman. She'd not only lost her daughter, it had created a family rift.

'And what does your brother do for a living?'

'He's manages a metal foundry. Two of my sons work with him.'

Kal nodded. She needed to get out there and start digging. In fact, she was itching to get started. Kal felt the woman's reluctance to let her go.

'I promise I'll do my best, Mrs Stanislova.'

Mrs Stanislova was weeping. 'You're very kind. You're one of the few people who've actually said they will help me.'

It was wretched leaving her like that. Kal gave the woman's hand a last squeeze.

Yes, she wanted to get going straight away. She must get out there and work the field, and the agony of Ivana's mother would only make her more ruthless and unstoppable.

Chapter Six

All Kal needed to start the hunt was one tiny clue. One little mark, or a sign, or an expression on a face which gave something away. That's all it would take to start the chain. And Kal knew she'd work all night and all day until she found that one tiny marker. Even if she had to question every single homeless person in the south west of London.

It would take more than ditching her money and her security to gain the trust of street sleepers. They'd know she wasn't one of them. Then again, they'd all started their life on the streets at some point and she hoped they'd have some sympathy and help her out. In fact, she was relying on it. No need for people to know she was perfectly capable of surviving on her own.

It was mid-afternoon. Walking along the Thames embankment, Kal shoved her hands deep in her pockets. Over on the other bank of the river, cafes and coffee bars were full, with their lights on and a warm glow coming from inside. A cold wind blew across the river and her stomach was already rumbling. A passer-by gave her a furtive look as they finished off the last of a hamburger and hurried past. The best way to look cold and hungry was to actually be cold and hungry, so that was off to a good start. Going undercover relied on immersing in the role.

One luxury she'd allowed herself was a pair of warm, waterproof boots. She hoped it hadn't been an extravagance that would set her apart or attract violence. She'd have to see how that one panned out.

No money – check. No identity – check. She must work as quickly as she could. It would take time to sift through the mass of bodies sleeping rough. Time officer Morris didn't have. The clock was ticking.

Clarence House covered a large area south of the river Thames, so she started with the obvious haunts of the underground stations, then the bus stations, showing Jennifer's picture and asking around, scouting for any Polish people.

Hour by hour, she worked her way steadily across the map. London's street sleepers were as mixed a bag as the rest of the population. Kal couldn't allow herself to get side-lined by those in distress, nor manipulated by those who pretended to have seen Jennifer when she could see clear as day they were lying. Some who did that were simply lonely and wanted to talk, others saw her as potentially weak and someone they could exploit. Kal always moved on with a smile.

She tramped from underpass to underpass and from doorway to doorway, searching for the nooks and crannies where people sheltered. Most street sleepers gave her advice or pointed her on to the next spot they knew of. When she told them she was searching for a friend, they looked in her face and made their own assessment. People were used to making a quick judgement of strangers. Friend or foe? It helped them survive when they had nothing.

Kal got into a steady rhythm. She didn't spend too long with each person. It only took her a few seconds to realise they didn't recognise Jennifer and then she had to move on before she got snagged by their baggage.

A horrible low point came around one o'clock in the morning when she discovered a young man slumped comatose in a concrete tunnel. It didn't look as if other people slept there and he had no dog for company. Kal could almost feel his loneliness. There were no signs of why he'd lost consciousness and, though his breathing was steady, there was no rousing him. Running to a nearby kebab take-out, she yelled at them to call an ambulance.

He must have led a bleak existence down here, cutting himself off from other people. The young man only had two possessions – a sleeping bag and a stuff sack. Kal hesitated before she searched through the stuff sack, but she did it, in case she found a clue to his identity. It contained an assorted collection of trash he must have squirrelled away from his time on the streets, and one battered old paperback novel – a copy of Asimov's "I Robot". A bookmark showed where he'd got three-quarters of the way through.

Kal stayed with him for as long as she dared. Once she saw the flashing lights at the end of the road, she skedaddled, melting into the night before she got pulled in for questioning.

Over the next few hours her thoughts kept drifting back to him – who he was, why he was there. Did he have family? Was someone out there looking for him? What path had led him to that lonely tunnel? He'd be revived in hospital and then what would he do? She made herself imagine him finishing the book in a much nicer place.

It wasn't until a couple of hours after, that she got her first break. Around three o'clock in the morning, a woman twice Kal's age pointed a dirty fingernail at Jennifer's photograph. It didn't linger on the face, it hovered over her neck. Spinks had been clever and photographed Jennifer in her undercover guise. Jennifer was wearing a red and orange, flowery scarf.

The woman was certain she'd seen it. Not on Jennifer but on someone else.

'One of Liz's girls had it,' she said.

The woman explained Liz was an older woman like herself. Liz liked to take new girls under her wing until they found their feet on the streets.

Kal felt a flash of optimism. Her legs suddenly stopped aching and she felt a new rush of energy. She knew the facts – most attacks on street sleepers came from "ordinary" people – stabbings, sexual assaults, even drinks that had been spiked – the homeless were seen as an easy target. It made sense for women to stick together. And more experienced street sleepers often looked after the less experienced ones.

The woman pointed further west and Kal thanked her with a gift of half a cigarette which someone had given her earlier in the evening.

The underpass near Waterloo station was a dark, yawning hole like an open mouth. It was a perfect spot for escaping the wind.

At the entrance, a trail of green ran across the ground and the air smelled stale. Further in, the conditions were dry and people were dotted along the walls as dark blobs. Most were swaddled in so many clothes or wrapped in cardboard tunnels, so it was impossible to tell if they were men or women.

Kal let her eyes adjust to the gloom. She trod carefully past the sleeping figures, her footsteps echoing off the concrete walls.

Sets of eyes tracked her. She could feel them on her back, assessing her, sizing her up. She'd disturbed them.

'Come and cuddle with me. I'll keep you warm.'

'Over here, darling.'

Kal side-stepped the arm which made a grab for her ankle, and she skittered further into the underpass.

A man snickered.

'Shut up Trevor, and leave her alone.'

A kind voice called after her. 'Go in further and you'll find the women.'

The underpass curved around a bend and Kal stepped gingerly as the light dimmed. It didn't smell bad here only it didn't smell fresh either.

She made out a shape sitting against the wall. The person's hair was tied in two long plaits.

'I'm looking for Liz,' Kal said.

The figure with two plaits said nothing.

A mattress was pulled against the side and another woman lay on it. Kal could hear the sound of heavy snoring.

'Are you Liz? Can you help me? I'm looking for a safe spot to sleep.'

'What are you staring at?' The woman with braids was young, maybe in her twenties, and she had a sulky voice. 'We haven't got anything you want.'

'All I need is a safe place to sleep. I was told to ask for Liz.'

'She can't help you.'

With a flick of her wrist, the woman with braids motioned to the mattress. 'She's dead to the world.'

'Oh.'

Shit. This was the end of the line. She needed Liz alert and clear-minded, not slumped in a drunken stupor.

'Yeah right, and you're new, aren't you? They always send the new girls to Liz. Look at her, lucky bastard. Want to know how she got like that?'

The woman with plaits lifted her hand and titled back her head as if drinking from a bottle. As she made the motion, the red and orange scarf peeked out. Kal had to stop herself from launching forwards to grab it. Then it was covered again by clothing.

She thought quickly. The woman with braids was a moody sort. Could she risk asking directly? Likely that would make her clam up. She couldn't ruin this with a sledge-hammer approach. Far better would be to hang around until she found an opening.

'So that's you stuffed isn't it?'

The woman with braids got up and brushed past Kal, knocking her deliberately with her shoulder.

'If you're looking for a place to kip, you'll have to negotiate with me.'

'Ok-ay. So can I sleep here?'

'Only if you say "please".'

Kal put a few steps between them. The young woman wasn't dangerous, nor was she intoxicated. This was a little game to see if Kal was a soft target or might have money on her.

The woman grinned. 'Don't worry. I'm not going to hurt you. Just say it.'

'Please.'

'And only if you pay me.' She looked down and pointed at Kal's boots. 'With those.'

Kal glanced at the disintegrating trainers on the girl's feet. Shit. If she protested she'd make it known she could look after herself. The woman wouldn't have her guard down and that was vital if Kal was going to get information quickly. She'd have to suck it up and wear the girl's stinking shoes which would freeze her feet off. Damn.

Kal slowly bent to undo her laces.

'Don't be an idiot. You don't give away good stuff like that.'

Someone else had appeared on the scene. A woman a similar age to the first and wearing a woolly hat.

'I was only kidding, Cleo. Think of it as her first lesson in life on the streets. I didn't mean anything by it.'

'If that's true then I won't need to go mentioning it to Liz when she wakes up, will I?' said woolly hat. She turned to Kal. 'Never give good stuff away. Not for anything.'

Woolly hat stuck out her hand. 'My name's Cleo and this is Tilly. You can kip near us if you want.'

Kal hung her head. 'I feel a complete idiot. I don't know how the hell I'm going to make it.'

'Yeah, you're definitely green,' Cleo said. 'But hey, don't let it get to you. We've all been there. Nothing to be ashamed about.'

'The first night is the worst,' said Tilly. 'And I didn't mean anything, I was only fooling around.

Kal sniffed and she put a little shake in her voice. 'I'm Kal.'

'Don't be upset, we'll get you something to sleep on,' Cleo said. 'Go on, Tilly, you owe it to her and hurry up.'

Tilly scuttled off.

'Oh goodness, you're shivering. Come and sit with me,' Cleo said. 'Don't worry about Tilly she's not bad or anything like that. Tomorrow, you'd better stuff some newspaper inside your clothes to keep out the cold. I'll help you find some, if you like. I know a good place.' Cleo was smiling.

'Thanks.'

Kal sat on the end of the mattress and hugged her knees. Cleo didn't ask any questions and she supposed it was part of their code. Most of them must have stories they didn't want to share. They sat side by side, listening to Liz snoring.

After a while, Tilly came back dragging some cardboard. 'This is for you,' she said. 'Put it beside our mattress, and that way, you'll be safe. Us girls have to stick together, that's what Liz says. At least, that's what she says when she's not drunk.'

Tilly and Cleo laughed and Kal was surprised because she'd expected to find depression down here and misery, not camaraderie.

'Roll it up to keep out draughts,' Cleo said. 'Tomorrow you can stick with us to search for food. It won't be as bad as it seems and like Tilly said, the first night is always the worst.'

They were two ordinary girls. And they certainly weren't killers. Maybe they associated with harder types? Or maybe Tilly had bargained for the scarf in the same way she'd tried to get hold of Kal's boots? Kal couldn't wait any longer.

She pulled out Jennifer's picture and showed it, careful to watch Tilly's face so she could judge any change in her expression.

'I'm looking for my friend.'

Cleo and Tilly exchanged a glance.

'Isn't that the missing girl?' Cleo said.

'Yeah.'

'She's a friend of yours then?' Tilly said.

Kal sniffed and nodded. Tilly didn't seem anything except surprised and she didn't seem to have noticed the scarf. Then again, the light down here wasn't too good.

Cleo shook her head. 'Sorry but we haven't seen her.'

She sounded definite.

'I don't want to frighten you,' Cleo said. 'But your friend could be anywhere. It's dangerous on the streets. But if you stay with us you'll be okay. We know the score and who's who and all that.'

Tilly had gone silent and Kal pointed a finger, making sure her voice went squeaky with the accusation.

'But that's her scarf you've got!'

Tilly jumped to her feet. 'Don't by stu-'

Cleo snatched the photograph and then pressed her hand to her mouth. 'Oh my god!"

'Don't be fucking stupid!' Tilly shouted. 'It can't be!'

Tilly was both upset and furious and it took a few minutes for the situation to calm down. In that time, Kal knew both of them were genuinely horrified. The scarf was ripped away by Tilly's own hands and it ended up at Kal's feet.

'I swear I don't know anything about it,' Tilly said. She was wiping her palms around her neck again and again, as if she had traces of the missing woman on her skin.

'I believe you,' Kal said.

'Hang on a minute,' Cleo said, 'You're not police are you?'

That put the frighteners on them and Tilly started crying.

'Do I look like it? Of course not. Jennifer was my friend and I'm looking for her. And I think you'd better tell me exactly how you got hold of her scarf.'

Tilly couldn't get the words out fast enough. It had been given to her by an old boyfriend. A man called Vlad who she'd ditched because of his drug habits. He'd been trying to get Tilly back and he'd given it as a peace offering. Tilly had only taken it because it was pretty.

'I want to talk to him,' Kal said.

'He's not here,' Tilly said. 'I don't know where he is.'

Kal narrowed her eyes.

'Yeah but we can search for him,' Cleo said quickly. 'First thing when it's light. 'Cos we know the places he hangs out.'

She accepted that. The scarf would be so contaminated it wouldn't offer much forensic evidence. And a couple of hours rest would be enough to keep her going. As long as she could keep an eye on the girls in case they changed their minds and decided to scarper.

The floor was rock hard. Kal ignored it. There'd been no such thing as a comfort zone in her upbringing and she fell back on her training, willing herself to rest in this alien environment. It was important to conserve her strength for the hard work to come.

Tilly and Cleo were whispering together on the mattress but she couldn't make out what they were saying. The minutes went by. She was off the starting block and that was good but she needed to keep going as fast as she could. As soon as the sun came up, they'd track down Vlad. Kal half-closed her eyes, willing herself to rest.

'C-l-i-c-k'

She'd never forget the sound of her father's gun at her temple. Nor the sweat and fear which slicked her back.

In the pitch black of the bunker, David Khan had set her a task. Find him. Or he would find her.

Patches of grit peppered the concrete floor. By that time, she'd learned to be stealthy. She was good at it. Relished the challenge of moving without a trace. So silent. No breath, no current of air to betray her. How to track your target in the dark. How to prevent them finding you. Speed could be your enemy but it could also be your friend. Watch out because your mind could play tricks. Your own fears or your desire to succeed – they could both trip you up. Stability of mind, calmness, focus and a trained body – they were the keys.

She had been so close.

'C-l-i-c-k.' Her father's gun was at her temple.

The sound made her heart stop.

'Better than last time,' he said, his voice icy. 'Now let's do it again.'

Kal shivered as the memory faded. Helping Spinks would chip away a bit of her own pain, she was relying on it, just as helping people in trouble had done before. It gave her hope that she wasn't always doomed to be an outsider.

Cold seeped through the cardboard and into her bones and she turned her mind away from it and slipped into a light sleep.

Chapter Seven

She awoke. It wasn't completely dark because a little
light filtered from somewhere in the distance, making
the space around her gloomy. She saw she'd collapsed
beside some iron bars. In one freezing jolt, the
nightmare came back. Terror raced up her spine and she
forced down a dry retch. She scrambled to her feet. Then
she saw two other women staring straight at her, their
faces pressed against the bars of their own cells. Her
heart felt like it stopped.

'Please don't cry.' The woman's hair was matted
and she wore plain pyjamas like convict clothes.

'She's right,' the second woman said. She was a red-
head. 'All you're doing is wasting your energy.'

They looked messy and unclean, as if they'd been
down here for ages. Their faces were streaked with dirt.

'It's normal to be frightened,' said the red-head. 'We
were terrified when we first arrived.'

'I... I don't understand. I don't know what
happened? This... this can't be right,' she said.

'They've given you something which messes with
your mind,' said the woman on her left. 'It happened
the same to us. Bits of your memory will come back later
on.'

Oh god, they were right. She couldn't even remember her own name. She had no idea who she was or how she got here. A wild terror started to take hold.

The two women exchanged a worried glance.

'Breathe nice and easy.' The woman on the left said it softly. 'Try to stay steady. We can help you.'

'Wait!' Her chest was constricting like a panic attack. 'You told me not to talk. Why are we talking? You told me it was dangerous!'

The red-head laughed and it sounded so weird and out of place, like a person all mad and wrung out.

'Yeah, only Kirsten knows when it's safe to talk and when it isn't. Don't you, Kirsten?'

'Yes I do. Hey newbie, don't lose it. You've got to stay with us. If you're going to make it you've got to listen to what we tell you.'

Her chest felt so tight she couldn't breathe. The need to vomit came again and she gave in to it and doubled over. Then, from somewhere inside her, a strength rose up. It surprised her. She didn't know it and she couldn't remember it, but she must be a strong person. Pull yourself together, a voice said in her head, you're made of sterner stuff than this. She straightened up and wiped at her chin.

The woman on her left, the one called Kirsten, was nodding her encouragement.

'That's it. Look at me newbie and keep looking at me.'

'W- who are you?' she finally asked.

'See?' said the woman with red hair. 'I told you they'd bring someone stronger. I heard them talking about it. This one's got more stuffing in her.'

'Clever girl, Ruth. Being the favourite has some perks when you get to listen in,' Kirsten said.

'Shut up! I'm not the favourite, don't say that.'

Ruth started pulling at her own hair as if she wanted to yank it out by the roots.

'Hey stop that! I'm sorry, it was only a joke. For god's sake Ruth leave your hair alone!'

'I can't help it, I just can't help it.'

'Keep your shit together Ruthie. Come on now, you know you can.'

The woman called Ruth stopped. She wrapped her arms across her chest, trapping her hands under her armpits. Then she started rocking backwards and forwards.

She thought she heard Ruth humming, yes, Ruth was singing to herself and it sounded like a children's song – Little Boy Blue. Oh god, this was a madhouse. She'd gone crazy or had a mental breakdown and they'd brought her here.

'She'll calm down in a moment,' Kirsten said. 'Ignore her and listen to me because we might not have much time. First thing is you're not going to remember your own name, so I'm going to give you one. I'm going to call you "Delilah". Do you like it?'

Hysteria grabbed hold of her. This was ridiculous. 'That's stupid.'

'No, it isn't. I like it.'

Kirsten looked crushed. Oh god, these two were falling apart.

'All right, all right, yes I like it.'

Kirsten clapped her hands together. 'Oh good and when you remember your own name, which you will do eventually, you might want to stick with Delilah.'

As Kirsten's eyes slid from hers, it was as if a cold hand clutched at her heart. She didn't want to ask, and at the same time, she couldn't stop herself.

'Why not?'

Kirsten had a strange look on her face. 'You'll find out.'

Oh god, she didn't want to find out. What could be so dreadful she'd forsake her own name? A primal instinct told her the answer to that question was something she never wanted to know.

'W-where the hell are we? And what the hell is this?'

'Oh boy, you really are strong. Most newbies roll around sobbing and wailing for at least a few days,' Kirsten said. 'Now this is going to sound horrible and I can't say it any other way.'

Kirsten took a deep breath in preparation. Delilah felt like being sick again and she gripped the iron bars.

'This is a prison and you are a prisoner.'

'A prison?' Her eyes told her it was true and her mind refused it. 'Now listen, what the f-'

Kirsten suddenly jumped like someone gave her an electric shock and she quickly tapped on the bars with her fingernails. Ruth stopped humming and Kirsten dived to the back of her cell and out of sight. Before she disappeared, Kirsten hissed one thing. 'You can survive.'

And Delilah remained there frozen, her muscles refusing to move and with Kirsten's last, dreadful words echoing in her ears.

Chapter Eight

Vlad was tall, with sandy hair that hung in his eyes. He wore a long, black, shiny coat that gave him the look of a character from a science fiction film and he had a gaunt face and hollowed cheek bones which were most likely the result of his drug habit combined with lack of food. Kal observed him carefully. Vlad was working his way along a bank of bins, sifting through each one. The bins ran in a row behind a huge office complex. He didn't seem to be on a high.

'This is one of his favourite haunts,' Tilly whispered.

It was only the third place they'd tried and Kal considered it lucky they'd found him so quickly. *Tick-tock*, said the clock she had running for Jennifer.

'So much food is wasted from these offices it's unreal,' Cleo said into Kal's ear. 'We don't usually come here because it's on Samson's patch.'

Kal cut Cleo a glance.

'He's the local heavy and a supplier – meths, pills, poppers, that kind of thing. Not really the hard stuff. But everyone steers clear of Samson's patch.'

'Cleo, that's hard stuff as much as coke and crack,' Kal said.

'Yeah, well anyway, that's why Tilly wants rid of Vlad,' Cleo said. 'When Vlad uses, he can go right off on one, can't he Til?'

Vlad sounded like a typical yo-yoing user who couldn't kick his habit. According to Tilly, he was currently on a dry spell and trying to keep it that way but the temptations of being part of Samson's network were always too strong. Tilly knew he'd end up being sucked back.

As she walked across the car park, Kal noticed an office worker watching from one of the rooms upstairs. One world inside and such a different world outside, separated only by a pane of glass, Kal thought. The office worker moved away.

Tilly told her Vlad had a kind side. He was looking after a stray cat and her starving kittens, bringing the mother cat food every day and making sure the kittens stayed safely hidden in an old warehouse. But Kal knew Tilly was frightened of Vlad. Reading between the lines, Kal was sure he'd been violent with her.

When she got within a few feet, Vlad stopped rummaging and turned bloodshot eyes in Kal's direction.

'Fuck off,' he said. 'This is mine.'

Kal balanced lightly onto the balls of her feet and let her arms hang loosely by her sides. Vlad was both tall and strong. She didn't want to have to be in a combat situation with him but she'd better be prepared.

'Tilly told me to say good morning.'

He scanned the area behind her and Kal was relieved she'd sent Tilly and Cleo away.

'Where is she?'

'I wanted to talk to you about this.' Pulling the scarf from her pocket, she fluffed it open in the air. 'I hear you gave it as a gift.'

'So what if I did?'

'The so what is it belonged to the woman who's gone missing. Which means you're in one hell of a deep pile of shit.'

Vlad had made to turn away and now he froze. His two eyes turned in her direction and they didn't look friendly. Kal felt her heart accelerate.

'That a threat?'

'Actually it's an offer,' she said. 'You tell me where you got this and I'll not have you run in for dealing.'

His laugh was ugly. 'You're not the law. And you can't do anything to me, I've got friends. You're a little bitch and I could break your neck with one hand.'

'Is that what you did to Jennifer?'

Vlad clenched his jaw and took a step towards her.

'Because if you did I think, for one, I should let Tilly know, don't you?'

Kal was taking an educated gamble. Drugs – Vlad had the backing of Samson and Samson's network and he wasn't scared. The police – it was pretty clear Vlad didn't care about them either. No, it was the idea of Tilly that gave most leverage with this one. Because he wanted her back. Badly.

Kal let the idea of Tilly sink in for a bit.

Vlad could be a killer. He was the type to lash out with full force, and with his physique that could have fatal consequences. Whoever was responsible for the killings had been organised. They'd plotted and planned. Was Vlad the type to stalk? Was that why Tilly had become frightened of him?

A cold shiver skittered up her back. She made certain to keep her eyes on him. In case he snapped.

'I didn't touch that missing woman and I've never seen her in my life.'

Kal nodded slowly. Best not to goad him too much. 'So where'd you get this then?'

The scarf wafted gently in the breeze.

'Where the fuck did *you* get it?' His finger stabbed towards her face.

'Jennifer was a friend of mine and she was wearing it when she disappeared. No, no, don't try to pretend you don't know her name. Everyone on the streets knows her name. So, like I said, when I saw Tilly wearing Jennifer's scarf I had to tell her where it came from, and well… she didn't think very highly of *you*.'

Vlad began walking around the back of her and Kal went with him, moving to keep herself facing his chest. Her palms had gone sweaty.

'I think Tilly'd like it if you helped me out.'

Vlad rolled that around his brain.

His coat had a newish look to it, and his clothing had a certain, dark style to it, as if he took some pride in his appearance. It also suggested he had access to money. Maybe money from drugs?

'How'd I know you didn't steal it from Til?' he said.

'That's a good question, yes, she told me you were smart. Well, Tilly and I are friends. She told me about that cat you're feeding and her three kittens and how the little black-and-white one died the day after it was born.'

Tick-tock. Hurry up, we haven't got all day. Are you a killer, Vlad? Let's see what you're made of.

'You're gonna make sure to tell Tilly I helped out, right?'

Kal sensed the softening in him as another side to his nature showed itself.

'Vlad, you can count on me. I promise I'll tell Tilly everything.'

***

'And that's the truth, I swear it,' Vlad said.

Kal stared at the blackened patch on the tarmac.

According to Vlad, he'd been scavenging down the alley and found a heap of clothing someone had recently set on fire. He'd rescued the scarf with a stick because he knew Tilly would like it.

'And you have no idea who put the stuff here or set it alight? You didn't see anyone? You didn't hear anything?'

'Not a soul.'

Kal paced around the area. A few scraps of material were still stuck to the ground, and there were patches of carbon that could be analysed. Luckily, it hadn't rained so Spinks' team might be able to get something from it. It was better than nothing.

She stared at the man in front of her. Should she take him in? Would the police be able to get any more out of Vlad than she could? She doubted it. But who was to say it wasn't Vlad who'd set the fire in the first place? That it wasn't him who'd abducted Jennifer? Or had he been ordered to destroy her clothes by someone else?

All she had to go on were the little bits of information Tilly had told her. And her gut feeling about Vlad. *Trust your instincts*, said the voice in her head. Yes, at the end of the day all she had was herself and her own judgements to rely on.

Kal crouched and stared at the blackened patch. Vlad was watching her and trying to work out what she was thinking, trying to work out whether she'd put in a good word for him with Tilly, trying to work out what she really wanted. She could still smell charring from the fire and it was acrid at the back of her throat. Sometimes it was better to let the rabbit run and see where it goes.

She didn't look at him when she spoke. 'I think you'd better get out of here.'

And she let Vlad go.

Chapter Nine

Delilah stayed rooted to the spot as a dark figure walked towards her.

She stared, open-mouthed, shock trickling into her system and paralysing her. She was like an animal in the headlights staring back at an apparition – staring at a face that didn't seem human.

The figure wore a dark robe that hung to the floor and a deep, black hood. And where the face should be there was a mask. A black mask with white painted features and the features were a grotesque caricature of a manically grinning face.

Delilah's mouth was bone dry and any words she imagined she might say or even shout got stuck in her throat. Now she wished she'd hidden at the back like the others. The figure sucked the words and the thoughts and the courage right out of her.

The nightmare figure stooped and a tray slid across the floor and into her cell. She could smell the food.

And inside herself, Delilah felt like a little girl facing a night time monster. A fantasy figure come alive and come to kill you in your bedroom. Don't speak, she told herself, don't say a word, don't even breathe - then it might go away. You're behind the bars, it can't get you. It's not real. They were little girl thoughts.

She managed to hold on for a few seconds, then her legs buckled in terror.

Chapter Ten

The staff meeting was due to start at any moment. It felt strange being here as an imposter and Marty wondered if the others could see she didn't belong.

No, that was stupid, she told herself, there was no exposure to fear. The only fear was the killer. She tried not to let her mind wander to the idea that the murderer might be sitting in the room with her.

As for the job itself – her passion for health and well-being should see her through, and she'd spent years coaching younger members at her kung fu club, not to mention co-ordinating a top-level security team. Putting together a health education programme should be a piece of cake.

At normal times, she imagined Clarence House had a cheap and cheerful feel to it. In the entrance way, a local photography club had hung up the winners of its annual competition. The theme was London life and some of the pictures were stunning. What Clarence House lacked in resources it likely made up for with its easy-going atmosphere and community involvement. A board outside the lounge announced a morning cookery course to be run by the local Women's Institute and later that day, a reading and literacy group.

But today, when she'd arrived, Marty had felt an edge of tension in the air. No one was relaxed. The staff were all struggling to keep things going.

The hard plastic of the chair dug into Marty's spine as she observed her new team mates.

Beatrice, the centre manager, was sitting next to her. The woman was nervous. She kept pushing her glasses up her nose and shuffling her stack of papers and she'd cleared her throat several times already. Was it because of Jennifer going missing? Had the police investigation put the centre manager on a knife edge?

Beatrice finally called for quiet.

'Good morning everyone. I'd like to introduce you to our newest member of staff, Marty King. Marty will be putting together our health education program.'

Marty smiled at the group. Goodness knows what strings Spinks had pulled to get her into the vacant position.

There were nods and hellos from the others in the room – Frank, McIntyre, Miss Pringle and Inspector Ian Taylor.

Frank, McIntyre and Miss Pringle formed the core, full-time team. They supervised the use of the day centre and were assigned specific caseloads of those on the street and offered them support, for instance, in finding employment, or a permanent place to live.

Marty looked from one to the other, careful to make eye contact. They'd be assessing her and making their judgements. Deciding for themselves whether she was capable of taking on a job that had, in the past, been filled by a male member of staff.

The evening before, Kal had urged Marty to wear a tight t-shirt which showed off her abs and toned arms. She was glad now she'd given in to the idea and she noticed how some of them stared too at the contrast between the white t-shirt and her black skin. This was going to be a challenge on more levels than one.

Marty had done her homework. McIntyre was the most senior of the team. He was well liked by the older centre users. Frank was younger and had tattoos over his forearms and a bit of a biker image. According to Beatrice, Frank was popular amongst the younger men and the younger women too. As well as being a caseworker, Miss Pringle was the centre counsellor.

The other person present was uniformed officer, Inspector Ian Taylor. Clarence House sat on Inspector Ian Taylor's patch, and since Jennifer's disappearance he'd become a regular feature at the centre. Whilst the investigation was being handled by DCI Spinks, Ian Taylor's team were cooperating fully, though they didn't know about Marty's role, nor about Kal.

'Unfortunately, our second new member of staff, Sadie Tyler, has been delayed,' Beatrice said.

'Is she really delayed, or has she got cold feet?' Frank asked. 'I wouldn't blame her if she has.'

Beatrice ignored him. 'As you know, Sadie's joining us to set up the new mentoring scheme. She called to say there's a family crisis and she'll be staying in Brighton another couple of days. She expects to arrive this weekend.'

Beatrice pushed her glasses up her nose. 'Marty, would you like to kick us off by telling us a little about yourself?'

***

Afterwards, Marty hung around by the coffee machine.

Giving up her old job at Wimbledon Lawn Tennis Association had been more difficult than she'd imagined it would be. It had taken years to work her way up to Security Team Manager. Her division at Wimbledon had been responsible for detection of bugs and bombs year-round and also at the prestigious, annual Tennis Tournament. She'd been a confident team leader. Though Marty would never admit it to Kal, she'd spent a few nights wondering if she'd made a big mistake. But now, mingling with the staff, she got her first feeling it had been the right decision.

Marty's experience meant she could easily see Beatrice's team wasn't working well. In fact, the group dynamics were a disaster. She could be useful to this investigation after all.

The main culprit was Frank. He opposed Beatrice on decisions, he raised objections, in fact, any chance he got, he threw a spanner in the works, talking on and on and taking up the whole meeting. She'd got fed up with the sound of his voice and Marty had seen how Beatrice struggled to hold her ground. What Frank needed, apart from a good kick up the back-side, was a direct challenge. That's what Marty would have done and it would have shut him up. The problem being that wasn't Beatrice's style – she too much of a peacekeeper.

Talk of the devil, thought Marty, as Frank came up and held out his hand.

'Very pleased to meet you,' he said.

She couldn't miss his quick, up-and-down appraisal. Marty gave him back a level, neutral gaze. Clearly, Frank was the type to imagine himself as god's gift to women – how boring.

'Nice to meet you too,' Marty said.

'I hope we didn't scare you off when we talked about the disappearances, especially the most recent one. Any woman in her own mind would surely want to stay safely inside.'

'Oh, I'm up to date on all that and it doesn't bother me.'

'Well, if you ask *me*,' Frank said, as if preparing for another one of his monologues, 'that's probably the reason why there were so few applicants for your position. I have to say, and I hope you don't mind me mentioning it, I find it strange a woman would take the post. First off with all the missing women, I mean what woman in her right mind would want a job with that hanging in the air? And secondly, I mean, the health part okay, but how do you expect to carry out the fitness sessions? Isn't that going to be very hard for you?'

The condescending son-of-a-- .

'I don't see that as too much of a challenge,' she said coolly. 'Why would it be?'

Frank gave a forced laugh. 'Of course not, I'm sure you're more than capable of holding your own, isn't that what all you modern women are like?'

Marty held her tongue. It would be unwise to make enemies or put people's backs up, even if she'd like to. She was here to do a job and that meant getting on with everybody.

'I've plenty of experience and plenty of practice dealing with difficult clients.'

'You're going to need it, especially since you're the first woman we've had in the post.'

Like I didn't know that. Marty sipped her drink.

'I hope you haven't taken on more than you can handle. It's great to be all politically correct and hire a girl, but some of these guys we deal with are going to give you a very hard time.'

She decided to let the girl comment slide. Security at Wimbledon pulled in a lot of different disciplines – plenty of ex-forces and ex-police personnel, electronics experts and geeks. She'd gained the approval and respect of most of them and a lot of them had been much older than her. No, Frank had no chance of rattling her cage.

'Not that I'm trying to undermine you or anything–'Frank said.

As if.

'–you'd better let me or McIntyre know if any of the centre users are giving aggravation. They know the rules except they don't all stick by them.'

I think I can probably handle that myself. 'Thanks, I'll keep it in mind.'

Marty knew she shouldn't, but she couldn't resist the temptation of staring at Frank's waistline. He wasn't overweight, but that didn't mean he couldn't benefit from losing a few pounds. He was a bit past the age when he could rely on his youth to keep him trim.

Marty patted her own toned abs. 'Tell you what Frank, if you fancy a session in the gym, come downstairs and I can fix you up.'

And when he looked annoyed, she smiled to herself.

***

Marty tracked down Miss Pringle in the counselling area. It was a grand name for a landing and a quiet room on the first-floor. A settee and an easy chair were angled towards a window, which was where Marty supposed Miss Pringle's clients waited. The counsellor's door was closed, so she knocked.

'Come in Marty, come in. Goodness, have you come for a counselling session already?'

Miss Pringle had her radiator on full blast and the room felt uncomfortably stuffy. A pot plant struggled for life on the desk top. Marty wanted to keep the door open to get some air, but out of politeness, she closed it behind her.

'Er, that's not why- '

'I'm joking! Though I wouldn't blame you if you felt like leaving after that dreadful meeting. What a horrible experience for your first morning.'

'It was pretty bad, wasn't it? Things don't seem to be going well.'

'That's diplomatic of you, only let's be honest – it was a disaster area. I shouldn't say it but sometimes I feel like whacking my colleagues around the side of the head.'

Marty laughed and caught a blast of Miss Pringle's perfume at the back of her throat.

'I've only got a couple of minutes before my next client, but take a seat. You've got to believe me when I tell you we're not always like that. We've been a tight-knit team but I think all these terrible… mutilations, are getting to everyone.'

'I guess that's human nature. When I found out, I almost didn't take the job.' Marty leant forwards and then wished she hadn't when she got another wave of scent. 'And please don't tell anyone I said that. Especially not Frank.'

'My lips are sealed. And as for Frank! He was out of order.'

'You can say that again.' Marty smiled. 'And I was wondering, is Miss Pringle…?'

'… really my name? Believe it or not, yes. I'm often snacking, you know – crisps, hula-hoops, and, of course, pringles. So it kind of stuck as a nick-name too and no one bothers to call me by my first name anymore.'

Marty nodded and found herself running out of polite conversation. She wondered how far she should push. With Jennifer's life in the balance, surely she should risk a tiny bit more? She could sense Miss Pringle was about to get rid of her.

'Glad you decided to stick around, and, as I said I've got my next client in a few minutes so…'

She decided to take the plunge. 'Maybe this isn't protocol, but I couldn't believe the way Frank was gunning for Beatrice. That was insubordination. Why didn't she put him in his place? I was dying to do it myself.'

'You'd think Frank would put their differences aside what with all the difficulties at the moment. But hey, some people don't let up on grudges, do they?'

Marty gave the counsellor an expectant look. 'Sounds like there's background.'

'Where there's conflict, there's *always* background. Frank wanted the centre manager job and they both applied and Beatrice got it. It's pure jealousy. Now with that poor volunteer going missing, Frank acts like it's Beatrice's fault, which is, of course, utterly stupid and very immature.'

As Miss Pringle spoke, she gesticulated with her arms and Marty caught a quick whiff of something rank. It surprised her and she wondered if Miss Pringle noticed, because the woman took out a small bottle and blasted more scent onto her neck.

'There can be a bit of a smell in here sometimes,' Miss Pringle said. 'From the clients.'

'Er, right.'

So why don't you open the window?

'Anyway, getting back to Frank. All Beatrice needs to do is stand up to him,' Miss Pringle said. 'McIntyre, who's got more patience than all of us rolled together, said he can see her losing her grip.'

She pulled a packet of nuts from her desk drawer.

'So that's all there is to the Frank and Beatrice story. Mind you I'm not holding my breath until that one blows over. Before you go, would you like some of these, or is it against the rules for you health types?'

They looked like her favourites only Marty didn't feel like taking any. The packet was already opened which meant Miss Pringle had already delved a hand in there. The sweet smell was getting to her and she wasn't entirely sure the underlying odour came from the clients, to her mind, it had come from Miss Pringle. How odd.

***

On her way down the stairs, Marty spotted Inspector Taylor and Frank chatting by the entrance. It looked like they were old buddies and they didn't give her a second glance.

Running down to the basement, she unlocked the doors to her new domain. A small office backed onto a large room which could be used as an exercise area or to house small seminars.

She'd decided she was going to run some drop-in sessions to meet the users and introduce herself. The first one would be yoga and the second would be circuit training. She'd make the second one gruelling and she'd make sure to participate herself, just to show them what she was made of and to get the word around she knew her stuff. Then over the next few days, she could start making plans for bringing in experts for sessions and talks – foot health, drugs, dental care – the works.

Marty was carrying a pile of yoga mats back to the room, when she noticed a light shining from under a door further down the corridor. She stopped and suddenly realised how quiet it was down here. And how remote from the rest of the building. As far as she remembered, there was nothing much down the corridor except a broom cupboard.

Long and dimly lit, the corridor suddenly seemed menacing. As she let the mats slip to the ground, her breathing rate picked up. Come on Marty, she told herself, don't let yourself get spooked. It's only a light.

Of course she realised there might be danger inside Clarence. But now she couldn't get the thought out of her mind. Stop it, she told herself, someone has simply come down here to fetch something and forgotten to turn off the light. End of story.

The most sensible thing would be to run back up and get Taylor or Frank to come down here and check it out with her. Thing was, if it turned out to be nothing, what impression would that give? Marty tried telling herself she didn't need to prove anything to anyone, least of all Frank, but it didn't do any good.

On tip-toes, she started inching down the corridor. The light was a thin band under the door. As she got closer, she thought she could make out muffled sounds from the other side. Her pulse spiked. It didn't sound like a machine. Were they human sounds? Or an animal?

She stopped. Still time to get help, she told herself. What if there's a body in there? Don't be silly, the murdered women were found on the streets. And dead people don't make a noise. The other possibility was the killer waited on the other side. But that was ridiculous. Or was it? What if they lured women into a trap?

A cold, irrational fear began crawling up her back. She'd only been here a few hours and the atmosphere was already undermining her cool, level head. This was ridiculous. Marty reminded herself she was no coward and a kung fu Black Sash and that this was most likely something as harmless as a mouse. Reaching out, she touched the door handle, then quickly shoved it down all the way and yanked the door open so hard it tore at her shoulder.

Half hidden amongst the buckets and the cleaning supplies, Beatrice crouched on the floor.

***

'I feel like such an idiot,' Beatrice said.

Marty had helped the centre manager to her feet and guided her out of the cupboard. They now sat side by side on a pile of mats in the training room. Marty handed over some tea and Beatrice blew her nose for the millionth time, before gingerly taking the mug.

'I've got no right to ask, I know,' Beatrice said. 'Only please don't tell the others. You can report me to the committee as being unfit for work if you want, only please don't tell the team. I'd never live it down.'

Marty ran her hand through her short, close-cropped hair. It had taken a few minutes for her own nervous system to get back to normal. Finding Beatrice had come as a nasty shock. At first she'd been panicked that Beatrice had been injured but it turned out she was simply crying her eyes out, hiding in the cupboard. It was strange, only not as strange as finding a dead body.

'Why would I want to tell anyone? You were upset and you wanted a safe place to cry. Listen, you know I left my old job because of work pressure. We've all been there. Things get too much sometimes and I know how that feels.'

'You're too kind, Marty. Your first day at work and you find your manager curled up bawling her eyes out, hiding in a cupboard… What must you think of me?'

'I think you've got a lot on your shoulders and you're probably worried sick about the murdered women.'

Beatrice started crying again. 'It's horrible. I keep expecting another body to turn up. I can't sleep. I have such horrible nightmares.'

'Have you thought of taking time off?'

Beatrice made a sound that was a strangled sob. 'Frank would love it. I'd be handing him my job on a golden platter.'

'Well, I've got to be honest, I mean it's perfectly obvious he's totally got it in for you. That staff meeting was, well, something else.'

Beatrice took off her glasses and rubbed at her eyes, smearing her mascara.

'Listen Marty, I like you and I probably shouldn't talk to you like this but we're in a crisis situation, so you may as well know I got the centre manager job and Frank didn't. I'm not gloating or anything, it's just a fact. I've worked with him for years and I've seen him do marvellous things with young people. He can get them to open up and he's saved so many from ruining their own lives. I honestly don't know why he's behaving like an idiot. You've got to believe me when I tell you that's not him. Frank's changed. Then again, I guess we all have with these murders hanging over us.'

'You can't help being affected by it, Beatrice. That's normal for a caring and sensitive person. And you must be caring otherwise you wouldn't be doing this type of job.'

'Gosh, how lucky we are to have found you. On paper you've got bags more experience than you need for this post and it's really showing. It makes me embarrassed. You've turned up just when we need you.'

'Sure,' Marty said. 'And if Frank's changed recently, any ideas what that's about?'

Beatrice blew her nose again and avoided meeting Marty's eyes.

'I wish I knew.'

Marty kept her own counsel and remained silent. Clarence House was certainly proving to be interesting. The team weren't only in crisis, they were hiding something. She felt sure of it.

Chapter Eleven

Since that first time, the same nightmare figure had come with the tray three times and slid it into her cell. She didn't know why but she refused to hide at the back like the others, instead standing trembling and with a tiny shred of defiance. At least she'd managed to stay on her feet the last time. She was being bloody-minded and stupid and she didn't care. And she hadn't touched any of the food.

Part of her still refused to believe she was really here.

A more logical part of her thought that for sure the food was drugged. Thing was, she was getting so hungry she'd soon have to give in. Just like Kirsten and Ruth, who ate slowly and without protest.

She'd had plenty of time to inspect her cell. There was a simple bed. A private toilet that was semi-partitioned in the back corner. A small sink with a mirror above it. She'd stared at herself in that mirror, touching her own lips and eyes and eyelashes and trying to bring back the memories. Nothing had happened. Delilah felt like a blank sheet of paper.

Now she sat near the bars so she could be close to the other women. It was a comfort of sorts.

How much time passed before Delilah heard a noise, she had no idea. There was no way of marking time here. That would be enough to drive anyone to madness, she thought. And poor Ruth was certainly very close to crossing that line.

She'd already decided this time she'd screw up her courage and demand what the hell they thought they were playing at. What kind of sick game was this?

Kirsten and Ruth didn't want to tell her. All they said was to make like she was happy. That otherwise she'd be killed.

Their behaviour made it more frightening. It was the look in their eyes. The way Ruth's hands shook. In the deepest part of her being, Delilah knew this was something altogether more horrific than she could imagine. And Kirsten and Ruth knew the shape and the size of it and were terrified.

Delilah sat up a little straighter as she heard the bolts being pulled back on a door, somewhere in the distance. Then she heard those same slow, heavy footsteps coming in their direction. She trembled. Was it because the steps were so measured? Or was it because she could *feel* the terror of Kirsten and Ruth? Both of the other women had retreated to the far reaches of their cells.

Again, she could smell the food as the tray scraped across the floor. Despite herself, her stomach grumbled.

This time the figure did something it had never done before. At Ruth's cell it beckoned the woman forward. Delilah watched horrified as Ruth came to the bars and the door was unlocked. Meek as a lamb, Ruth stepped through and Delilah saw that she had a strange, fixed smile on her face. *Make like you're happy.*

Don't go, she wanted to scream. *Don't go with it.*

Ruth looked so frail as she followed the robed figure. A dread rose up from Delilah's gut. All she could hear were the figure's slow footsteps because Ruth was in bare feet. She wanted to scream at her to come back, wanted to scream at the figure to leave Ruth alone except nothing came out. Then came the sound of the far door being bolted from the other side.

She sat frozen in place, unable to move. It was a long time before she realised it wasn't complete silence like before. And from the tiny sounds she heard, she knew Kirsten was stifling her crying way back in the confines of her cell.

Chapter Twelve

Kal blended with the shadows, keeping back as far as she dared behind Vlad.

Her father had loved games in which he stalked her or she stalked him and Kal knew how to play it right, with careful positioning and a light presence. With Vlad, the difficulty was he kept to isolated streets and she had to be careful not to make any giveaway noises. At one moment, she made a mistake when her toe brushed an old tin can. It rang out loud and clear and she'd expected Vlad to startle or spring in her direction. He did neither, too caught up in his own head.

It was a relief when he moved on to busier places. Amongst other people, Kal melted into the shadows and the everyday momentum of those around her.

Within a few hours, unknown to him, she'd accompanied Vlad on his tour of the bins and watched four different interactions between Vlad and fellow homeless men. Only one of them was interesting.

Two men had approached Vlad and the little group headed off to a café. With steamed up windows and a radio blaring in the background, Kal took a seat out of their eyeline. Then she watched as the three of them ordered coffees. Their conversation seemed tense. One man gesticulated as if he were haggling. Then came the handing over of a package. It was done with a slick skill which only comes with practice. Vlad was wearing his usual long, black coat and he tucked the bundle into his clothing. Was it drugs? A payoff?

Did Vlad really have what it took to abduct and kill several women? She doubted it. Or was he a runner for a more powerful player, for instance, Samson? Was Samson not only into drugs, did he have other perverted activities involving killing young women?

An hour or so later Vlad knocked on the door of a terraced house in Battersea. He was inside for a few minutes and when he came out, Kal made a quick decision.

As Vlad crossed the road, she jogged and bumped into him. Vlad swore and swung around and she made sure she was fast heading away, her face tucked into her hood, hair tied back out of sight. Of course, she'd already changed clothes for the surveillance and she didn't think he'd link the incident with their earlier meeting. Traffic quickly flowed between them.

The collision was enough to tell her the parcel was no longer there. Which meant he'd left it inside the house. Spinks must add the address to his hit list. She was hoping he'd be able to set up permanent surveillance. After all, she couldn't be everywhere at the same time. Samson was a big enough fish to merit resources.

Kal followed Vlad until she discovered the location of the abandoned warehouse and the kittens. It was a derelict and unstable structure with big signs outside warning of the dangers. Vlad squeezed through the chain link fence and disappeared inside. Once he left, she did a thorough reconnaissance of the building. It was an old factory which had been abandoned and everything inside was in a state of decay but there was nothing of interest – no women's clothing, no blood and certainly no signs of an incarcerated woman.

She took a few minutes to confer with Spinks. His team was already at the burnt tarmac collecting the evidence and he told her whoever burned the clothes had good local knowledge because the CCTV footage in the area was pretty much non-existent. Shit. Just the bad luck they didn't need.

Tick-tock.

Kal weighed her options. The trail felt like it was going cold. Her priority should switch to Clarence House to try to pick it up again. She doubled back to find Cleo and Tilly.

***

Kal met up with the others down by the river and told them what Vlad had said about finding the burning clothes.

'They were Jennifer's clothes, weren't they?' Tilly said. 'He's got mixed up in something dreadful.'

'If either of you know anything about it, you'd better tell me.'

Kal gave them a hard look which made Tilly's tears start again.

'I absolutely swear I don't know a thing,' she sobbed. 'Vlad's not like that. He's not a k-k-killer.'

'And what about Samson?'

'Samson's a right bastard,' Cleo said. 'All I know is to steer clear of him. Liz told us to.'

Tilly was looking at Kal with big, wet eyes and Kal made herself ignore the doe-eyed look. She was here to squeeze for information and these two were her oranges. She must press right down to the pips.

'Do either of you use the centre down the road, Clarence House? I want to know everything there is to know about it.'

'Clarence? Oh yeah, I go there sometimes. They do an all-day hot breakfast,' Tilly said.

Cleo shot her a disapproving look.

'What? Nothing wrong with that, I'm in and out, I don't hang around,' Tilly said defensively.

'Liz doesn't approve of Clarence House,' Cleo explained. 'That's why I *never* go there.'

When Kal said she wanted them to take her, Cleo wasn't playing ball.

'I will,' Tilly said, and she got to her feet. 'What Liz doesn't know can't harm her. Liz says Clarence House has a bad *vibe*.'

Tilly exaggerated the word and she tried for a smile, not pulling it off because her mind was still churning over Vlad and the scarf.

'It's not funny Til, Liz isn't just some old drunk, she always says what she says for a reason,' Cleo said.

Which made Kal even more eager to get there.

***

With a red brick frontage and large, old-style windows, Clarence House was a bit run down. Yet what it lacked it made up for on the inside, with a spotlessly clean, lino floor and a cared-for interior with colourful photographs on the walls. A huge yucca plant had pride of place in the entrance, its leaves polished and without a speck of dust.

On the ground floor, Kal and Tilly joined a queue in the canteen for a free bacon sandwich and a hot drink. Then they ate staring out the window. Sharing the canteen with them were around twenty other people. Some sat alone. Others chatted in groups or played cards. The room had the distinctive odour of unwashed bodies and unclean clothes.

Kal saw no signs of anything amiss amongst the volunteer staff serving the food, or amongst the centre users. Though the atmosphere was sociable, Tilly wasn't comfortable and she ate her sandwich fast, cramming it in as fast as possible.

'Let's get out of here,' Tilly said. 'If you want a look around, I'll take you on a quick tour before we go up to the showers.'

They passed through a communal lounge with sofas and a giant, flat screen television. The room smelled faintly of bacon from the kitchen next door and a few people slouched watching a news programme. In the corner, a group played table tennis and at the far end, a police officer was playing pool with a bunch of men.

No one had paid them much attention since they'd walked in the front door. No one had made eye contact with Kal and only the volunteers had spoken to them. So it was odd how the officer's eyes tracked Kal and Tilly as they crossed the room. Kal felt the hair on her arms stand on end.

Tilly pulled Kal close. 'That's Inspector Taylor,' Tilly whispered. 'Don't look at him, keep walking.'

Kal waited until they were out of the lounge and half way up the stairs.

'What's up with the Inspector?'

'He's a creep. Steer clear of him.'

Kal decided she'd get the most out of it if she played naïve. 'But's he's a policeman! He's one of the good guys.'

Tilly gave her a pained look. 'Don't be stupid. If I tell you to not go near him then you'd better listen. My friend Fiona showed me a *huge* bruise on her neck from where he'd grabbed her with both hands.' Tilly lifted her hands to illustrate a strangle hold.

'You're kidding me.'

'I'm not. The word is he's gone in heavy on a few of the girls. Followed them and stuff. He even took Fiona to his house except she got away. So keep well out of his reach.'

'Didn't she report it?'

'He's the police stupid, he can do what he wants. Who's she going to report it to? Mind you, she told me he has a nice house over on the Woodside estate. She took me to see it afterwards. Seems like he's a motorbike fanatic. He's even got a Hell's Angels thing painted over his garage door.'

They reached the top floor landing.

'Yeah and Fiona's no air-head. She probably thought she was gonna get something out of going with him but it didn't pan out that way. He scared the wits out of her. She thought he was going to rape her.'

'Shit!'

'What? You wanted the gossip, didn't you?'

'Taylor might be involved in the killings.'

'Are you crazy? He's a brute but he's not a psychopath, you've been watching too many movies. Come on, let's go for a shower and I'll show you the laundry room and the facilities. There's hot water and soap and you can use them for free. There's even a new health program – hygiene and all sorts, if that's your thing, and I hear they've got a woman for once. Maybe *she'll* turn out to be the killer.' Tilly snorted. 'Come on Hercule Poirot, you'd better wise up if you want to find your missing friend.'

After the tour, Kal had a feeling Tilly wanted to get rid of her and she let herself be ditched. It suited her, because she wanted a word, on her terms, with Inspector Taylor.

In any investigation there are dead ends. There are frustrations. And there are opportunities which must be identified and followed up. This was one of them. Kal ran back down the stairs.

Taylor was still playing pool. Kal noticed how he'd positioned himself so he had the best view of the room and the door. It was a cop's instinct. Despite his concentration on the game, between plays, Taylor's eyes habitually swivelled to take in the room. Another cop habit. And it meant he was pretty sharp at his job.

It took him no time at all to clock her entrance. He would know she wasn't a regular. He would see she didn't speak to anyone and know she'd come with Tilly. Kal wondered how much hanging around she'd have to do to make him want to come over. As it was, it didn't take very much.

For a while, Kal watched television and picked a couple of young guys to flirt with. She laughed at their jokes and did a few sexy wiggles. Taylor was watching her, she knew it. She stayed for a few more minutes, then left the room.

Inspector Taylor caught up with her as she was heading out the front door.

'Excuse me,' he said. 'I'd like to speak to you.'

Kal turned. Taylor was stocky and solid. His hair was dark brown and short, and the skin on his face was rough, as if he scraped it every day with a kitchen knife rather than a razor. It gave him a menacing look. Inspector Taylor wasn't smiling.

'I'm Inspector Taylor. I wonder if I might ask you a few questions. We're conducting an on-going missing persons enquiry.'

'Oh, you mean about Jennifer.'

The man held a lot of tension in his chest and shoulders. At the mention of the missing woman's name, Taylor couldn't hide his eagerness. Like a dog who's picked up a scent, she thought.

'That's right,' Taylor said. 'Did you know her?'

'Not really.'

'Except you knew her name.'

Kal shrugged. 'Everyone knows her name. It's the only thing being talked about.'

Taylor moved towards her and took her arm to steer her around the corner and out of sight. Then he crowded her space and Kal backed up against the wall. He was starting to remind her of a pit-bull – short and powerful, with a nasty bite.

'It's a very important police investigation. Lives might be at stake.'

She nodded and she let herself go limp and passive as he pressed towards her. He was very close. On his breath, she could smell what he'd had for breakfast. She could see dry patches around his mouth.

'If you met Jennifer, it would be best if you tell me everything and anything you know.' Taylor was gripping her forearm with one of his meaty hands. And now he squeezed.

'I d-don't know anything. I n-never met her.'

Kal twisted her face to the side and the Inspector took her chin with his other hand and forced her to look straight at him.

'You sure about that?'

Taylor squeezed the flesh on her arm harder and pinched her chin.

Of course, she wanted to knee him in the groin. Adding to the temptation was the fact he was positioned perfectly. Kal held back. Keep your discipline and act the part, she told herself. Let's see how far he goes. Let's see what's underneath that uniform.

He had a coarseness about him that made her want to recoil. Taylor was close enough to kiss her and for a moment she thought he might. Then he pulled back.

'You hurt me,' she said, rubbing the red marks.

'Is that so?' Taylor said it with a sneer, and he marched off back to the lounge.

The bastard. Kal watched him go. Yes, Inspector Taylor and you're certainly not the stable, reliable officer that Spinks described. She'd found a rotten spot. Time to dig a little deeper.

Chapter Thirteen

The estate with Taylor's house lay a couple of miles from Clarence House. Kal took a bus ride straight over.

A couple of turns of the housing estate were enough to identify Taylor's place because the biker logo over the garage made it impossible to miss. Now, would Inspector Taylor live alone or would he have a partner? Since he'd brought Tilly's friend back here, Kal doubted he had a partner or lodger. No, she was pretty certain Taylor was a loner.

A quick peek through the back windows confirmed it. This was a bachelor pad – with grey tiles and unwiped, grey surfaces in the kitchen, minimalist, with no knick-knacks stuck to the fridge and no clutter. In fact, hardly any colour in the place at all.

This was a neat and trim neighbourhood with cut hedges and small but tidy front yards. The type of estate where retired people might be home during the day. The neighbours at the front had too good a view for her to risk entry there and the house had double glazing and, most likely, dead locks throughout. The man was security conscious, she'd give him that.

Kal smiled to herself. Then she put her hand in her pocket and took out a pair of black gloves and Ian Taylor's keys. With him pressed against her at Clarence he'd been easy to pick pocket. And she'd been lucky because he kept his keys in his front right pocket, like with most right-handed people.

Most likely he wouldn't realise for several hours and by then she'd have done her work. Even if he did miss them, Taylor would have no idea she'd lifted them. All she needed to do was drop them on the floor somewhere at Clarence and some kind soul would hand them in at reception. She had no hang-ups about going in. This is what she was on this case for – to nose around and scratch about and do the stuff Spinks couldn't.

The back door to the kitchen opened soundlessly and Kal listened for any tell-tale noises – a television or a radio, or the floor creaking upstairs. All she heard was silence. She closed the door and shouted out.

'Anyone home?'

There was no scuffling of surprise or stealthy footsteps, or someone scrambling and tripping over themselves to make an emergency phone call. Good.

The downstairs lounge confirmed her view Taylor was a bachelor. Take-away remains were strewn across a table, and the place stank of fish and chips. In the corner of the room, a pile of white shirts and a couple of pairs of trousers had been slung over an ironing board.

The downstairs didn't hold any nasty surprises. There was nothing of any note and certainly nothing to raise any suspicions about his character or interests. It made Taylor look like a perfectly normal male. Of course, that didn't mean he was.

Taking the steps two at a time, Kal ran upstairs, the pile of the carpet masking her footfalls. She kept her arms lightly balanced away from her sides, ready should she encounter trouble. But there was none to be had. The upstairs was as deserted and uneventful as downstairs. She didn't even find any pornographic magazines, nor evidence of drug use, prescription or otherwise, in the bathroom cabinet. Inspector Taylor might be clean after all. Though that didn't explain his over-the-top behaviour. He'd overstepped the boundaries in a big way and he'd done that for a reason. She needed to dig until she found out why.

Kal retraced her steps to the ground floor. There must be a clue here and she had to find it. The only place left was the garage.

Working with her father hadn't made Kal cynical about people, rather it had opened her eyes to the secrets people hide. She knew the lengths some will take to deceive those close to them, and she knew the elaborate mind games people played to deny the reality of their crimes to themselves. She wasn't searching for dirt on Taylor, she only wanted to know the truth about who he was, in order, perhaps, to cross him off her list. Her interest wasn't personal against him, this was professional.

A serious looking lock adorned the door at the back of the kitchen. Kal had seen it on her way through and now she made herself stop to understand why, with a lock like that, it hadn't been the first place she checked. Because you only put on a lock like that if you didn't want anyone going inside. Or getting out.

Kal stood still and made herself reconsider her earlier choices. Well, she'd wanted to make sure there was no one else in the house and that was always a priority.

Be honest with yourself. Yes, that wasn't the whole reason because she'd been pretty confident the place was empty. No, she'd avoided the garage because of loyalty. In some way, her loyalty to Spinks and her belief in him had stopped her from checking the obvious first. Stopped her from finding out the worst about Taylor first. She'd wanted to put off the inevitable by a few seconds. Kal spoke sternly to herself. That was a way to get herself killed. That was a way to get Jennifer killed. She must *never* let another person influence her actions. Independence must always be her first priority.

She took a breath. And wondered if in the next one she'd smell decomposition and a rotting corpse.

The key turned easily and Kal pushed open the garage door.

It was dark inside. As she let her eyes adjust, Kal took a deep breath and smelt engine oil. In the dim light, she made out a motorbike in the middle of the floor. Along the side ran a workbench with a scattering of tools and more hanging from an array on the wall. On the floor was the metallic plate for a mechanical jack, indicating Taylor was a serious motorbike mechanic.

Should she flip the light switch? Yes, why not. In the temporary dazzle, she felt the kick of adrenalin as her body registered the moment of vulnerability. Kal kept alert and quickly scanned her surroundings. In the corner was a type of wooden shed, a bit like a Swedish sauna – all pine wood panelling and a compact size.

So what's your secret, Mr Taylor? She said to herself.

Walking to the cabin, she found the door locked. The key was the second one she tried on the bunch in her hand. And as the door to the sauna swung open, Kal had to steady herself on the doorframe.

Lurid, disgusting photographs stared back at her from the wall.

Taylor had pinned up giant crime scene photographs of the mutilated women. The corpses were caught at different angles and each section of the wall concentrated on a different body part – torso and breasts, slashed wrists, bloodless face, eyes. The images were graphic and made her stomach clench. Kal put her hand to her nose as if she could smell the bodies, though there was no odour.

This was sick. Only a professional coroner or pathologist could have a display like this and it be deemed normal.

Underneath the photographs, Taylor had pinned hand-written notes. They were scribbled on lots of small bits of paper with ripped edges. The overall impression was of chaos, not order, as if someone had written them in a manic frenzy. Oh god, the man was deranged.

Bending to the notes, she read confidential information about the location of each body, the time of discovery and other vital bits of police intelligence.

Kal took out her mobile phone. As she took careful shots of the walls, she searched for any tiny, incriminating piece of information, such as a personal comment, or a slip up that gave away Taylor's prior knowledge of a death, or a personal connection with the victim.

After a painstaking hour, she had to admit she'd found nothing that linked Taylor to the murders. All of this seemed to have been taken from the police dossier. And anything that wasn't from the dossier was Taylor's speculation about the killings after the event.

Yet it spoke of a troubled mind. Or an obsessed one, or a mad one.

Kal put her phone back in her pocket. How best to handle this? Was it the right moment to confront Taylor? Or inform Spinks?

The level of disturbance here was serious. Taylor wasn't stable. But was this the mind of a serial killer? It felt as if the key to it all was actually missing but could she risk letting it run for a little without doing anything? It was dangerous to have a man like Taylor on the loose. It was like inching closer and closer to the edge of the cliff to try to see more of what was below. But if you got too close…

Spinks was right – this case had a very bad feel to it. And Kal had the impression she'd not got to the bottom of the stinking barrel yet. Not by far. She was only chipping away at the edges.

Sitting on the floor, she made herself check and double-check her strategy. She even listened to her father's voice in her head, which she only did in a dire emergency. Then she locked the cabin and left Taylor's house exactly as she'd found it.

Chapter Fourteen

The second-in-charge has gone away for a while. He's meeting with our new Brother in America. Which means I'm left to fetch and carry food for our guests.

They like hammering home it's me who's the servant. They didn't even bother to say what a great job I did finding the new guest, no, not one single word of thanks. Ungrateful bastards. Sometimes I hate them.

We all follow the strict rules of The Lodge. The rules which were laid down at the beginning, whenever that was. We must not ask questions, and we must follow blindly. It's like I'm suffocating under piles of regulations.

The masks sit gleaming on the rack. I know I shouldn't touch, not unless I'm told to. Thing is, since I'm on my own, no one's going to know, are they?

It's porcelain and heavy and I have to be careful because my hands are shaking so much I might drop it. The thought of it shattering on the floor fills me with terror. If anyone ever finds out I've accessed the guests without permission, I'd be severely punished.

I watch in the mirror as I place the smooth contours over my own face, brushing back my hair so all traces of *me* are removed. The heavy cloak and hood conceals the rest. This is what makes it safe to be someone else. That's the power of what we do. That's why we do it. To be someone else. To be someone or *something* raw and primal.

I know I shouldn't have a favourite, but with her red hair and beautiful voice, she's always been the one for me. Today, I'm going to take my chance. After all, her days are numbered.

In the mirror, I look the part – the grinning face ready to laugh with his playmate.

Whilst the basics of our practices are archaic, there have been a few modernisations. For instance, the glass shower cubicle, though I don't remember who had the idea of installing it. Whoever it was, they were a genius.

Her wet hair streams down her back and I sit and watch. The mask hides my admiration of her body. And the heavy cloak gives me an authority and bearing which I lack in real life.

I've seen how our guests cower. That's what I love about The Lodge because it sets us apart from ordinary, stupid people scurrying about their boring, everyday lives. We are better. We have power way beyond their imagining.

Ruth steps out of the shower and begins to slowly dry herself. I think she's become immune to our observation, though I can remember how, at the beginning, she cringed and shivered and tried to hide herself. Now she's learned better.

I remind myself that, at the moment, I am in charge. That I have decided to take this opportunity alone with her and that she will comply. Of course she will.

I've laid out a dress and I watch as she slowly steps into it. It's lavish and silky and falls to the floor, showing her off in her splendour. It was to be saved for Ruth's final ceremony. Ruth turns her lovely back to me in a silent request. Naturally, it's all done without words and with a smile, because she knows to do otherwise will risk a punishment. The whip is my Brother's favourite, whereas I prefer the stun gun.

I step forward and my fingertips caress her skin as I close the fastening. As she turns to face me, I see the quivering of her bottom lip. The excitement of it thrills me.

I've organised a banquet for the two of us. It's an intimate dinner, at which she will play the part of my perfect, adoring admirer. Later she will sing for me.

This is what I like the most, well, that and the fear and watching others at it. The others prefer more barbarous acts. For me, it was always voyeurism and my brother allows me to get away with playing it that way and he covers up for me. Without him, I'd probably never have been allowed to continue as part of it all.

Our table awaits and Ruth takes my arm. As I lead her through to the adjoining room and pull out her chair, I can't help it but part of me feels melancholy. I suppose it's because of her decline. Her terrible loss of weight. How she shuffles like an old woman. My poor Ruth.

I watch her dine and there's a knot in the pit of my stomach because they always choose the weakest. That's why I'm taking the risk of this stolen evening together. You see, I'm pretty certain Ruth won't survive much longer. I think she will be the next one picked.

Chapter Fifteen

A triangle of grass with a few trees and a couple of benches was all it was. You couldn't call it a park, though it was a nice spot, right opposite Clarence House and perfect for watching the entrance.

Kal sat in the spring sunshine. It didn't bother her that Taylor was a police officer. The bigger problem was how to handle the bleak discoveries at his house. If he were implicated in the killings, she'd need more than a bunch of photographs to tie him in. That's why she was cutting Inspector Taylor a bit of rope – to see what he did with it.

At the back of her mind sat the unthinkable. What if more members of the police were involved? It would be one explanation for why the killer had evaded justice so many times. She left that unexploded bomb sitting at the side. The clues were starting to point towards an organised group and she was clear on her priority – which was to get them all, whoever they were.

It wasn't long before Kal realised she wasn't the only one observing the comings and goings at the day centre.

A man, fairly short and thickset, with thinning hair and probably in his forties, was watching the entrance from the other side of the park. He wore a purple waistcoat and was partially hidden behind a fir tree. He seemed to be taking snapshots of everyone who came and left Clarence House. There was something in his posture and manner of movement which told her he might have a learning difficulty.

Kal spent a few minutes watching. She was rewarded for her patience when someone exited Clarence and headed straight across the park. She recognised him from the files – it was Frank, one of the caseworkers.

At the fir tree, Frank spoke to the person taking the pictures and laid his hand on the other man's shoulder. It was a dominating gesture, given Frank's height. Then Frank passed over a small item. Maybe it was sweets, because she saw the shorter man remove a wrapper and put something in his mouth. A few minutes later, Frank returned to Clarence.

Being in the right place at the right time was an art, some said. Kal didn't know if she thought it was an art or luck, though seeing the detail around you was definitely an expertise. And this was a detail she definitely wanted to examine.

She came around the other side of the tree and took him by surprise. It made her feel bad, because now they were up close, it was clear the man had Down's syndrome.

'Hello, what are you doing?' she asked, keeping it friendly. 'My friend just went in there. Why were you taking photographs of her?'

He regarded Kal and didn't say a word.

'I'm not accusing you.' She shrugged. 'I heard it was a strange place, that's all. Is photography a hobby of yours?'

He finished off his bar of chocolate and brushed a few crumbs from his waistcoat. He nodded. 'Is it a hobby of yours?'

'Yes, can I see some of your shots?'

She put her hand out in the hope he might pass over his phone. He didn't.

'Have you got any chocolate?' he asked.

'Not on me, though I could get some. My name's Kal, what's yours?'

'Dougie.'

A young man came running up. 'Hey, Dougie, how'd it go? Time to pack up and head back home. Oh, is this a new friend?'

In one hand, the new arrival was carrying a take away cup, and in the other, he had a small bar of chocolate. He positioned himself between Kal and Dougie.

'Hi, I'm Simon. Is everything okay, Dougie?'

Dougie nodded, his eyes intent on the chocolate.

'Here you go mate.' Simon handed over the bar, shook hands with Kal and then gave her an expectant look.

She presumed Simon was Dougie's helper. He had a protective stance and acted brotherly, though he was certainly not Dougie's brother and was some twenty years his junior.

'I saw him taking pictures of my friend when she went inside.' Kal indicated Clarence House with a jerk of her head.

'Dougie doesn't mean any harm. If you like, we can show them to your friend when she comes out and if she wants, we can erase them, can't we Dougie?'

Dougie shook his head.

'Yes we can Dougie, you remember we talked about that? About respecting other people's privacy?'

'Oh, I don't think Tilly will mind, I just got curious about what he was doing.'

Dougie was busy munching. 'I'm waiting for my girlfriend,' he said.

This sounded so unlikely that Simon gave Kal an apologetic grin.

'Dougie had a special friend and he lost touch with her,' Simon said. 'She used to come here and, well, we often wait here to see if she might have come back.'

Kal felt her attention crystallising on every word Simon said. 'Was she a street sleeper like me?'

'Her name was Ruth, and yes, she was homeless and she was a busker.'

Ruth was the other woman on Spinks' list, the one who'd gone missing some twelve months before Ivana.

'Dougie got lost one time down by the river and Ruth helped him find his way home. She came by the house a few times after that and started playing guitar first for Dougie and then for the other residents. Ruth became quite a feature, especially on rainy days because there was always a spare meal after she'd led a singing session. She was a great musician, really talented.'

Simon gave a good-natured laugh. 'We all miss her. Dougie especially.'

Kal smiled back. 'What happened to her?'

Simon's eyes glanced off Dougie. 'Oh, I don't know, she was a wanderer, so I suppose she took off some place. Ruth was a bit of a rolling stone, wasn't she Dougie?'

Simon spoke gently for Dougie's benefit, not for hers. 'We reported it to the police and none of the girls they found fitted Ruth's description. That was a big relief, I can tell you.'

Simon's words were important – he'd told her Ruth was talented. Wait a minute. Ivana wanted to be an actress and maybe she really did have a gift for it and Ruth was a musician. Could this be a link? Could it be the beginning of a pattern? There was something important here, she knew it.

It turned out Dougie did have Down's Syndrome, and he lived with several other residents in a group home. Aside from Simon, there was a small team of helpers who took turns providing support for them.

Kal played the part of the new girl on the block and Simon knew a lot about the itinerant community because he'd worked in a shelter. According to Simon, many street sleepers had no real family to turn to. They were used to moving on when problems came up – be it debt, addictions or bad experiences. This made it impossible for anyone to know what happened to Ruth. Dougie listened to everything and said very little and she supposed they didn't get many visitors, because both Dougie and Simon were happy for her to tag along.

She followed them all the way back to the group home, which was a cosy house with a couple of bicycles chained outside, presumably belonging to the staff. Early daffodils were growing in huge tubs in the front and when she went inside, there was a big vase of them on the lounge table. It gave the place an airy, bright feel.

They showed her video footage of Ruth singing for the residents. Kal's attention spiked again. Like Ivana, Ruth was an attractive young woman. She had long, wavy red hair and gorgeous green eyes. But most startling of all, she had a lovely voice.

Dougie stared at Kal without blinking for a long time and then he wanted to show her his comic book collection. After that, they scrolled through picture after picture on his phone. Kal found herself warming to him. Maybe it was because she had the habit of being guarded around everyone she met and with Dougie it wasn't necessary. The half hour she spent with them passed pleasantly and helped keep at bay her mounting concerns with the case.

Kal certainly didn't want to deceive Dougie nor give a false feeling of being his friend. The thing was you could never predict someone else's reaction and Dougie seemed to have made up his own mind that he was Kal's new friend.

As she relaxed, Simon gave her a knowing smile.

'Dougie either brings out the best or the worst in people,' he said. 'He's extraordinary really.'

One thing was clear, Dougie had adored his busker friend. Kal could see he hoped she might be some kind of replacement. Simon saw it too and he pulled Kal into the kitchen to help him make cheese on toast.

'You mustn't take advantage of him,' Simon said.

'I wouldn't do that,' she said. 'I'm not that kind of person.'

'I didn't think you were, it's just Dougie is still hurting even though Ruth went missing over two years ago and he's very trusting. He doesn't always see the complications in life. He likes you and I think it's because you remind him of Ruth.'

With people like Dougie and Simon, she didn't need to push and probe, it would be disrespectful to them and it wouldn't get her what she wanted anyway. They were ordinary, nice people and if they had useful information about Ruth, they probably didn't even know it.

'We're both street girls, so I guess there's a connection between me and Ruth and,' she gave Simon a sharp look, 'we're both rolling stones.'

'I get what you're saying and don't worry, I'll talk it through with Dougie later. But I don't think that's the reason he likes you. Dougie is a good judge of character. I think he likes you because you're kind. Remember I told you Ruth brought Dougie back when he was lost? It was pouring with rain and plenty of people must have walked straight past Dougie even though he was upset. It was Ruth who took the trouble to help him and it took her a long time to find this place and by the time she got him home, they were both soaked through. That's the similarity you have. You're kind, just like her.'

No one had ever called Kal that in her life.

Simon laughed. 'Took the wind out of your sails, didn't I? Dougie can see straight through your hard woman act and get right to the soft core.'

He leaned forward. 'Don't worry, we won't tell anyone.'

When Kal went to leave, Dougie gave her a bear hug.

'You'll come back won't you?' he said.

'Yes, Dougie, I'll visit you again.' And she meant it. It had been good for her to come here and be reminded of what an ordinary life was, with music and friends and flowers, and cheese on toast. Right on the doorstep, a surprising little question popped into her head.

'What did Ruth say when you last saw her?'

'She told me to wish her good luck,' Dougie said.

Kal felt a funny prickling at the back of her neck.

'Oh, that's interesting,' she said casually. 'Did she tell you why?'

Dougie had a stubborn look on his face and he shook his head several times.

***

That night, Kal lay alongside Tilly and Cleo's mattress.

Ruth had plans. Secret plans she'd asked good luck for. There was more to this than a single, sick killer snagging girls off the streets at random. And the more she discovered, the more she felt certain they were dealing with an organised group.

In here was a pattern. A pattern that meant Ruth and Ivana had been targeted. These girls were beautiful and talented and they'd been chosen for a reason.

Kal spent a cold and troubled night.

Chapter Sixteen

In the silence, it felt as if insects crawled up her back. Her scalp prickled and her skin itched. Delilah scratched and squirmed, even though she knew there was nothing there. It was a nervous reaction. Or maybe it was the drugs they were putting in the food. In the end, she couldn't stand it any longer.

'Is it safe to talk?' she whispered.

Kirsten didn't stir from the back of her cell.

'Kirsten, for god's sake answer me.'

'Yes, it's safe to talk. Is that good enough for you?'

An image of Ruth's bare feet flooded Delilah's mind, and Ruth's soft footsteps as she followed the cloaked figure. She felt the words jamming in her throat. She daren't ask, and at the same time, she *had* to know. She forced herself to blurt it out.

'Where have they taken Ruth?'

Kirsten came to sit at the bars of her cell. She had swollen eyes and Delilah caught a glimpse of a deeper pit than sadness, something more like despair.

'I knew you'd want to ask questions.' Kirsten rubbed her nose on her sleeve. 'I'll tell you most of it. Though there's some stuff I don't want to say out loud.'

'All right.'

'It's not I don't want to help you, it's just you've got to understand talking makes it more real and much, much worse. I just can't say the words. It's better for you to find out for yourself little by little. Otherwise… ' Kirsten shook her head, ' …otherwise...'

The look of despair came back. Delilah pretended not to notice.

She tried to swallow and she couldn't, her mouth was too dry.

'Where has he taken her?' She whispered it.

She called the person a man due to the height and build, though Delilah realised it could have been a woman behind the mask.

'Ruth went with the mask.'

Delilah nodded and she saw how Kirsten was clenching her fists.

'I don't think it will be the worst. When they take you, there are little clues you can look out for to guess what's going to happen. Plus I think it was the same person who usually brings the food trays. If I'm right, it means this time Ruth will be taken to wash her hair and put on make-up and dress up in something expensive. There's a candle lit dining table and mouth-watering food and you have to sit opposite and make like you're having the time of your life with your devoted partner. That's what that one likes.'

Kirsten's voice was dripping with sarcasm and part of Delilah registered it as a good sign. It meant Kirsten hadn't been broken yet.

'There's wine. There's goddam classical music in the background. With him, all you have to do it act the part. Ruth told me he once stroked her hair though that one doesn't usually touch you.'

Delilah's mind knew this meant there were other people and other situations where they were touched. She shoved that information out of the way and spoke to stop her thoughts from going there. She said the first thing that popped into her mind.

'How can he eat with his mouth covered?'

'He doesn't. He sits and stares and you've got to carry on as if everything is normal. The first time it happened to me I wanted to smash the wine glass and get him in the neck. Or grab a knife and stick in it him. Thing is, if you do any tiny thing they don't want there are punishments.'

Kirsten turned and lifted her shirt. Two lines of red, knotted scars ran across her back. It was like in horrible pictures from the days of slavery – as if she'd been whipped. Delilah stared in horror.

'Later Ruth will have to sing, and by that time she'll be naked. When it's with him, no one else is there. With the others… it can be more than one of them… and… worse stuff happens.'

Delilah let the silence hang. She hugged her own chest with her arms.

'There are little signs to look out for so you know when you leave here what you'll be facing. Maybe you can prepare yourself. I'm going to teach you. It's important.'

Delilah stared dumbly. The pieces were coming together in her mind. Oh god. This wasn't a mad house as she'd first thought, though likely she might go crazy like Ruth. No – *mad, crazy things happened to them*. It crashed around inside her head and she could see blood, and Kirsten screaming as she was whipped, and masks with a cruel soul that would make her do terrible things.

This time it was Kirsten who stayed at the bars and it was Delilah who crawled to the back of her cell. On her bed, she hugged her knees, like a tightly curled foetus, with her eyes closed, trying to squeeze out the horror.

Chapter Seventeen

Zipping up her jacket, Kal nestled far back to get maximum shelter. The Windmill café was a popular, outside meeting place for joggers and nature lovers. Slap bang in southwest London, it sat on Wimbledon Common which covered some four hundred and fifty hectares of brush, open common and woodland.

She had on the same set of clothes she'd been wearing on the streets for the past few days and her appearance didn't appeal to the other clients. Aside from looking like a tramp, probably she smelled like one. It was ironic to think how people might be worried about their purses and handbags. She noticed a couple of women clutching them extra close simply at the sight of her.

Marty jogged along the footpath, wearing a wind-proof top that looked so cosy, Kal couldn't help eyeing it with envy.

'Wow, you look terrible,' Marty said.

'And it's great to see you too.'

'Yeah and sorry I'm late,' Marty said. 'I was talking to a couple of the girls at Clarence. I didn't want to break off the conversation.'

'Sounds interesting.'

'It's straight down to business then is it?'

Kal shrugged. 'That's the way the cookie crumbles on an investigation.'

'I got you, and yeah, they're a strange lot. The street girls are wary but at the heart of it, a lot of them are really young. I'm building bridges.'

'Of course. That's your gift. Give me everything you've got. And hurry up and get in some hot chocolate, won't you? And how about food? I'm freezing and we've got a lot of ground to cover.'

'You're the boss,' Marty said.

The aromas at the Windmill café were stronger than she'd ever known them to be. While Marty was at the counter, two women came to sit at the next table and one of them shot Kal a suspicious look. In return, Kal gave her such an unpleasant glare that the woman flinched. Serve her right, thought Kal, for sleeping in a warm bed and being self-righteous.

While she talked, Marty tucked into a huge falafel and houmous hot baguette that made Kal's mouth water. She'd already finished her beans on toast and she watched as a blob of houmous thunked onto the table and she had to sit on her hands to stop herself from scooping it up.

'The biggest break is a rumour about Frank. What I heard is he got a someone pregnant and it was hushed up.'

A slice of tomato fell to the table and Kal didn't bother to restrain herself. She swiped it up.

'Hmmm, delicious. Was she under-age?'

'No, though I was told she was on the young side and she was a client at the centre. Any staff-client

109

relations are strictly forbidden. Frank should have lost his job, or at the very least, been suspended.'

'Right. So why wasn't he?'

'Don't know yet. And no one's linking this to the disappearances and I haven't got the name of the pregnant girl. I'm not sure if it's important or not? What do you think?'

'I think you'd better hurry up and finish that damn thing before I tear it out of your hands. Listen, everything is important. Don't rule anything out.'

'Okay.'

Kal tried to keep some of the intensity out of her voice, though she was pretty sure she failed. 'And what about Inspector Taylor? What's the vibe on him?'

'He gets on well with Frank and with McIntyre. The three of them hang around together. I suppose that's normal given Inspector Taylor has practically taken up residence at Clarence since Jennifer disappeared. Apart from that, nada.' Marty gave Kal a sharp look. 'Why?'

'No flies on you, Marty. Don't get caught alone with Taylor. He's threatened clients and he did it with me. There's something nasty going down with him.'

Marty stopped chewing. 'Shit.'

An image flooded Kal's mind of the first young woman in Spinks' trail of victims. The giant crime scene shot on Taylor's wall had shown the woman's naked limbs, her flesh almost paper-white against the tarmac. Kal shivered.

'I took a look around his house and no, don't ask me how.'

Marty closed her mouth.

'Taylor's got a nasty habit of collecting pictures of mutilated women. It doesn't prove he's a psycho but it could mean he is. This is something big, Marty. People on the streets are scared. You just told me how you felt nervous going to check the light in the cupboard and people are feeling exactly the same – jumpy and jittery.'

'I can't put my finger on why it's getting to me. The atmosphere at that place is damn weird.'

'Right. You've been infected by it and you should take notice. Listen, an individual can justify in any number of a hundred ways why they had to kill someone. The thing is, at the end of the day a killer is a killer – that's how I see it.'

Kal was weighing her words carefully, not wanting to scare Marty and not wanting to sugar-coat it either.

'An organised group – that's something entirely different. In a group or a society, people stoke each other up. They play on each other's fantasies. They egg each other on to go further. A group is altogether a different beast to an individual and much more dangerous. Remember that when you're at Clarence.'

A sudden coldness stole into Marty's blood. She cupped her hot chocolate and looked across at Kal. Her friend was the type of person who could take on other people's depraved acts and not be sunk by them. The type of person who could use a person's acts to profile them, just as her criminal father had taught her. For the first time in her life, Marty felt thankful, in a small way, for David Khan, and even more thankful she had Kal by her side.

Kal shelved telling Marty her real fear. The one involving Spinks. Would he turn out to be a betraying, criminal bastard, just like her own father? Was he involved? The police were well known for their membership of secret groups, especially members of the police in the upper echelons.

Kal could feel a dark storm rolling closer. She'd soon find out, and would it be the end of her fragile belief in the good and the righteous? The end of her belief in good men like Spinks. Was everything in life completely fucked just as she'd once believed? She knew she'd have to fight to not be dragged under when that one broke. And she didn't want to go back to living in the shadows again. She shook herself out of it.

'We're getting into very dark waters. You still okay to carry on with the assignment?' Kal asked.

An organised group? No wonder she was getting the heebie-jeebies at Clarence, Marty thought. Any number of them could be involved. And if Ian Taylor was part of it, Kal was right, they were treading in dangerous territory.

Marty lifted her chin. 'Of course I am.'

Chapter Eighteen

Sadie Tyler made her way to the checkout, tucking a small packet of chocolate biscuits into her basket.

Why not treat herself? Coming to London was a fresh start. Away from the long-term boyfriend who had cheated on her with her so-called best friend. Away from her colleagues, who'd known all about it and felt sorry for her.

She'd lost weight for him, hadn't she? Gone to the gym and joined an aqua-biking club so she'd look better in a swim suit for their summer holiday. Well, now it would be for her. She'd carry on with her regime for herself, not to please someone else, and certainly not in a bid to keep them. A new start was exactly what she needed and the position at Clarence House had come up at the right time.

Sadie exchanged a smile with the woman at the till and packed her items into a bag.

The street was full of traffic and Sadie decided she couldn't be bothered waiting for a bus. Walking home would be good for her. A walk would also be a great way to get to know her new neighbourhood.

She passed a cinema, three take-away outlets and a second late-night grocery store. The scents from the Indian take-away were enticing. She'd definitely be coming back to try that one later in the week. This was a decent area. She could be happy here. Of course, it would take a while to find her feet and make new friends, and she had to admit she felt a tad nervous at the thought of her new job. Setting up a mentoring scheme from scratch was a lot of responsibility.

She'd been feeling waves of anxiety about her first day for a while now. And with it looming tomorrow, she knew it was getting the better of her. Sadie tried some positive self-talk, repeating on a loop how she'd got the qualifications and loads of experience, and she knew her stuff. In a couple of weeks she'd be laughing at herself for being worried.

The positive-speak helped a bit. Later she'd phone her sister and get a little pep-talk.

Away from the main drag, the road was much quieter. The woman in the flat opposite had mentioned a cycle path cut-through. She said it made the walk much quicker than going the long way round and Sadie had followed her new neighbour's advice and taken the cycle path on her way to get her shopping.

Now she stopped at the entrance of it. The path was a long, thin stretch of tarmac with two borders of cut grass and the backs of houses on either side. It must have gotten much later than she realised because looking down it now, daylight had already faded. Street lamps threw out weak pools of light but Sadie noticed how the pools didn't really connect.

The grocery bag was cutting into her fingers and Sadie stopped and put it down. She hesitated. That was the problem when you didn't know an area, you had to

114

learn the unwritten codes and where was safe and where to avoid.

Had there been muggings here? Was it safe to go that way when it was dark? Wait a minute, she told herself, this isn't a high crime area, it's a decent neighbourhood full of families and working couples who could afford their own place. That's why she'd chosen it. Her friendly new neighbour wouldn't have told her about the cycle path if it wasn't safe. Sadie took out her phone and checked the local map. From what she could see, going around would take about three times as long and that shopping bag was getting ridiculously heavy. Come on Sadie, she said to herself, don't be a chicken.

***

The Lodge never leaves any loose ends. That's how we've continued undetected for so long. You see, our activity passes beneath the radar. It's swallowed up in the noise made by the missing young women of earlier decades, who were always presumed to be runaways or mentally disturbed. More lately, our activity has been hidden by high numbers of missing street drug users and alcoholics, presumed vanished I suppose, or simply dropping off the bottom of the social pile into oblivion.

Ahead of me, one of those loose ends we never leave is walking home carrying her groceries. Sadie Tyler can link the parts of the puzzle together. Though she doesn't realise, she knows about our past and she could bring it all crashing down. Coming to London onto our new patch is the biggest mistake she's ever made.

Earlier on, Sadie had a jaunty stride. It's as if the woman was excited. As if she's on an adventure and the local high street holds the promise of evenings to come, and that these shops are going to become her new best friends. Of course, I know better.

I check my watch. I am the one who has been chosen to do it.

In the supermarket, I waited patiently as Sadie made her selections. No one gave me a second glance. It's because I'm so ordinary looking and they're all busy, rushing towards their Friday night schedules, getting ready for the weekend ahead.

Then, out she came with a heavy bag. I already know where she lives. And I'm waiting for my best opportunity. If necessary I'll take it inside her flat, though I'm hoping that won't be necessary because it would be more difficult to make it look like a nasty accident.

The noise of the high street fades as we enter the side streets. She walks down a line of respectable houses. A long row of cars are parked for the night and the shadows are nice and deep. Around us, curtains are already closed for the evening and there's no one in sight. This is all perfect. I wait in the dark as Sadie thumbs her phone. Perhaps she's lost. Will she turn back to the high street and decide to get a cab? That would be the most sensible option. The safest. Naturally, it would also narrow down my window of opportunity.

The grocery bag slumps on the pavement for a few moments before she picks it up again and makes for the direction of the cycle path. Oh yes, my luck is in. I get the cord out of my pocket and hold it in my right hand. Taking a quick look around to check no one's come into view, I follow her down the alley.

***

Sadie was almost half way when her nerves got the better of her.

This was a big mistake and she knows it because someone has followed her. The hairs on the back of her neck are standing on end and she speeds up, at the same time telling herself she's being silly. Pull yourself together, she tells herself, it's simply another normal person on their way home, not some rapist. Only she daren't look behind. In case. Best to get to the other end as fast as possible.

It's a long stretch, much longer than she remembered on the way there. Sadie can hear her own heavy breathing and it isn't from the exertion of carrying the shopping. Her heart is beating hard and she tries some more self-talk to try to calm down. This time it doesn't work. She still tries telling herself it's her imagination and she's over-reacting and the part of her which wants it all to be normal prevents her from flinging aside her shopping and running as hard as she can for safety. Also, she knows she's not a good runner. In a fumble, she remembers her phone and her hand is shaking so much she can hardly dial. The footsteps are coming closer and she dares a glance. What she sees scares her so much she drops the phone. There's a small tinkle as the glass breaks.

Trying to scream and kick at the same time, Sadie twists against the tightness around her throat, as a dark figure pulls her to the ground.

Chapter Nineteen

Light rain fell from a grey sky onto grey tarmac. Underfoot, the ground was slippery as Kal hurried towards the crime scene. The nights sleeping rough were starting to take their toll. She badly needed to go back to her apartment and warm up with proper food and a hot bath and then a duvet but she wasn't going to allow herself the privilege.

Up ahead, a melee of professionals clustered outside a cube-shaped, white tent. The crime scene crew were working hard to preserve what remained of the evidence, before it got washed away by the weather.

A young officer stood at the yellow and black tape-line.

'You can't go this way, miss, the cycle path is closed. You'll have to go around.'

'I'm here to see Detective Chief Inspector Spinks. My name's Kal Medi. Please can you let him know I've arrived?'

He opened his mouth to object and then thought better of it. The fact she knew Spinks' name was enough to make him do a swift re-evaluation of her. Good for him, she thought, he had the makings of a good policeman.

Inside the closed-off area, another officer overheard them speaking and when he turned, Kal recognised Inspector Ian Taylor. Ah, this was going to be interesting.

Rain dripped from Taylor's peaked cap. Likely he'd been here for some time getting wet and he didn't look very pleased to see her.

'Don't I know you from Clarence House? What are you doing here?'

'Same as you,' Kal said, cutting to the chase. 'I'm here to inspect the crime scene.'

The authority in her voice threw him right off balance.

'Here to inspect-!' Taylor almost choked on his breakfast. 'You cheeky-'

Kal was sorry to see Spinks approaching at a fast pace, his stride long and purposeful. She'd been looking forward to a few more moments enjoying herself at Taylor's expense.

'Now, now Inspector,' Spinks said. 'Kal is perfectly entitled to join us because I invited her.'

Struggling to contain himself, Taylor's cheeks literally went purple and Kal couldn't help it, to egg him on a tiny bit more, she gave him a beaming smile. It almost made up for the concrete floor and the hunger and the damp. She felt the hardships melting away like butter, as she watched Taylor contort himself to keep control.

Spinks put his hand on Taylor's shoulder. 'Let's go inside Ian, and I'll fill you in on the details'

Using that as a description was a bit of an exaggeration. Blocking out none of the noise and not all of the weather, the tent acted as if it might blow away at any moment.

A woman lay face down, her dark hair plastered to the pavement. A nasty mark on the ground was all that remained of a blood stain.

A team of technicians were working painstakingly over the ground, searching for evidence, and they all paused to take in Kal's appearance.

'Kal is working for me,' Spinks explained to Taylor, and in a voice loud enough for everyone to hear. 'That's all you need to know. And you're just in time, Kal. We're about to turn the body.'

The three of them moved closer.

'She was found by a shift worker at two o'clock this morning,' Spinks said. 'Cause of death appears to be strangulation. Her valuables are missing. Thanks to Inspector Taylor, we have an early identification of the victim as Sadie Tyler.' Spinks gave Kal a heavy look. 'She's a social worker from Brighton and she was due to start work at Clarence House.'

When she received Spinks' brief summons she'd expected to be coming to another exsanguinated victim. This was a new turn of events.

Taking a slow tour of the body, she noted the way the limbs were sprawled. Whoever had done this had been on top of Sadie. They'd strangled her from behind, and from the abrasions around the neck, a cord or rope had been used, not hands. Sadie's clothing was intact, indicating there'd not been a sexual motive. She listened as the pathologist filled her in on his findings, which concurred with her own.

'That's a lot of violence to get a handbag,' Kal said.

Spinks and the pathologist both nodded.

From their manner together, the strong working relationship between her and Spinks would already be obvious to everyone, though Taylor seemed to still be fighting his disbelief at her involvement. Doubtless he had plenty of questions about Kal that Spinks had already made abundantly clear he wouldn't be answering.

They stepped aside as the pathologist and an assistant gently rolled Sadie onto her back. Apart from a bruising of the lips, the woman's face was intact, which indicated the attacker had not smashed the victim's head into the ground to subdue her – they'd had sufficient weight and strength to not need to do that. With the body in this direction, it was clear one of the woman's arms had been broken – indicating extreme force had been used. Again, that would be highly unusual for a standard mugging. Most muggers only wanted the item of value. They weren't killers. Muggings only went wrong if someone retaliated and if the mugger carried a weapon and was prepared to use it. For someone in good health, death was not a common result of a street theft.

A camera flashed as the technicians took new shots. Kal noted the last few details of the body and the little markers on the floor that indicated how Sadie's shopping had spilled as she was brought to the ground.

No, this was a targeted murder, she was certain of it, and she felt sure Spinks thought the same. And she didn't believe in coincidences. This woman had a connection to the killings.

Kal was kneeling, and when she stood, she stared Taylor straight in the eye. How long would it take for the crime scene photographs from this death to find their way onto Taylor's wall? What was the payoff for him? Was it a mental and emotional kick? Or was Taylor part of a more complex plan? Inspector Taylor returned her gaze and he didn't flinch. From his reaction, she could draw no negative psychological conclusions – no obvious discomfort, no guilt and no giveaways. At least, not for the time being.

Spinks had higher rank and she saw how Spinks was relaxed around Taylor and how Spinks shared information freely. In fact, Ian Taylor seemed to be an indispensable part of the team.

Spinks was giving Kal an odd look. He must guess she was scrutinising Taylor. Too bad. He'd brought her in as an independent and that's what being independent meant. Spinks would have to be prepared for the consequences, however close they fell to home.

'Time of death estimated by the pathologist as close to midnight,' Kal said. 'Where were you at that time, Inspector Taylor?'

He went blue at the gills and she wondered if he might lose it completely and punch her, right here in front of everyone.

'What the hell!' He was choking on his own words.

'Answer the question please, Inspector Taylor,' she said evenly.

'How dare you! I don't have to answer *to you*.'

He looked at her like she was something the cat dragged in. Be careful Taylor, she thought, don't be fooled by appearances. Kal watched him carefully – watched his eyes and the tension in his face and the way his neck was knotted.

She stepped closer. This was the moment to squeeze out more.

'Something tells me you get a kick out of these deaths.'

Taylor almost burst a blood vessel – a man with a short fuse, a man who routinely used force against the centre users, someone obsessed with the killings. *Come on, Inspector, what more are you going to give away?*

He came towards her and it was Spinks who broke them apart. Spinks took a firm hold of Kal's arm and pulled her away.

'Taylor's a good man.' Was the first thing Spinks said, once Taylor was out of ear-shot.

No point in not coming straight to the point, she thought. She and Spinks had too much mutual respect, or used to have she thought grimly, to not be direct.

She shook off his grip. 'What makes you so sure?'

Spink's clear grey eyes bore into her and she reminded herself what an astute and experienced detective he was.

'If you've got information to share then I'd appreciated being kept in the loop,' Spinks said.

He wouldn't be fooled by her fobbing him off. And doing so wouldn't solve Sadie's murder nor the murder of the other women. How much to tell, that was the question.

'Inspector Taylor has lurid photographs plastered over his garage wall, with all the victims blown up large.'

She thought Spinks swayed a little, although when he spoke, he did it with an authority which she felt in her bones.

'Do you have proof?'

'Yes,' she said.

'And what else?'

He'd hit the problem on the head.

'Nothing so far.'

They stared at each other for a good few seconds.

'That's not enough,' he said.

She knew that already.

'Are you going to take him in on it?'

'On what? Bringing his work home with him?' Spinks snapped.

'It's much more. It's sick. And it's against protocol to-'

'I know what it is.'

Spinks had interrupted her and he was losing his patience. Or was it a ruse to throw her off his trail?

'Send me what you've got and leave it with me.'

So you can gloss it over and Taylor can cover his arse?

Spinks stared back at her. 'We raided the house you highlighted in Battersea. We got drugs and enough to

125

pull Samson in for questioning. But there was nothing to tie him to the killings.'

'Forensics on the charred tarmac?'

'Nothing so far.'

Shit. Another dead end. Or had Samson, Spinks and Taylor made it all neat between them?

When they went back to the tent, Taylor eyed her suspiciously and Spinks appeared so unruffled it seemed as if nothing had passed between them. Kal marvelled at his professional poise. And she reminded herself to keep on her toes.

'One witness has come forward,' Spinks said. 'I've already spoken to him but if either of you would like to meet him?'

'Of course,' Kal said, and Taylor indicated he would too.

The rain was stopping, leaving the alley washed-out. Kal tried not to think about the woman's final moments and whether or not she had suffered. The ticking bomb with Spinks name on it, she also left untouched. Kal disciplined herself to concentrate on the facts and the information at hand. It was the only way she could help Sadie now.

The witness was a teenager. He wore baggy tracksuit trousers and a sweatshirt with a geeky joke on the front. He happened to look out his bedroom window at the right moment to see a cloaked, hooded figure entering the alleyway. The figure had been wearing a mask.

'You saw a cloaked, hooded figure wearing a mask.' Taylor repeated the information from the statement sheet. 'Did you think to mention this to anyone at the time?'

The boy shrugged. 'There was no one to tell because Mum and Dad were out. And anyway, why would I? It's not a crime to get dressed up is it?'

Spinks was standing back and letting Taylor take the lead.

'Did this person give you any reason to believe they were a danger to others?' Taylor asked.

'No, it was odd, that's all. I didn't think anything of it until I heard the sirens.'

Kal felt pretty certain the boy was telling the truth. His face and mannerisms told her he wasn't lying or exaggerating for effect. He'd seen a figure dressed the way he described. Which *was* odd – and it was opportune, because for the other victims they had no witnesses. One more strange fragment to add to the puzzle.

After, Taylor hung around like a dog and that was interesting too. In the end, he had to be dismissed by Spinks.

'I'll check into Sadie's background,' Spinks said. 'You keep concentrating on the streets. We need to work faster.'

His hand had strayed to the eagle pin at his lapel, in the same way it had when Spinks first told her about the case.

'You're certain Jennifer reported nothing before she disappeared?'

'Are you doubting me? Come on, Kal, you know me better than that.'

'Do I? Just making certain.'

Yes, and how much did you ever really know another person? She hated to admit it, but she could sense a flaw in him. A scar connected to that eagle pin. And she didn't yet know its shape and form and what lengths it might drive him to.

'Nice pin,' she said. 'Where's it from?'

She wanted to ask him who it was from, but that would have been too pointed and would have shown way too much interest. This way it was more casual.

'Oh, I picked it up on holiday one time.'

The flick of Spink's eyes down and to the left told her he lied. Probably only a white lie, she reminded herself. Nothing to do with the case. He doesn't have to bare his life to me and goodness knows, I've not shared my own sordid history. And she tried to shelve the sinking feeling she felt inside.

It was time to carry on. She'd already decided she wouldn't be going back to the streets, not yet. No, contrary to Spink's directions, she wanted to look into Sadie's background. In fact, the way Spinks deliberately steered her away from Brighton and Sadie's past made Kal determined to go straight there.

Chapter Twenty

The lettering that's the trademark of The Lodge is written large on the wall. It's carefully positioned behind the catwalk. I look through the camera, making sure that when we capture live events, we also capture the blood-red writing.

It's difficult to concentrate. A few moments ago, Adam confronted me. He knows I took out Ruth when I had no right to. He knows we had a banquet and I used the special dress. Damn him. I cleaned up meticulously, but he knows me and he knows my habits. Perhaps he could see it in my eyes.

I'm working my way down my checklist. You see, it's my task to make sure the technology is glitch-free. It has to work seamlessly when we capture and beam out every moment of the Ceremony to our new Brother in America. He mustn't be disappointed.

Since I'm the one with the technical skills, I hope that means I'm safe.

It's due to me we have live link-up in the first place. Without me we wouldn't be able to reach out. Wouldn't be able to inspire others. It's my tech expertise which makes it possible. We've come a long way from those early days when Adam and I were first led into the barn to witness the unimaginable. Of course, I'm never given any credit. Ungrateful bastards.

My hands are unsteady as I check the wiring. The Grand Master would have to be told, that's what Adam said. This time he told me he couldn't cover it up, that he was sick of my weaknesses.

I've got away with it so many times. Perhaps I've relied on the protection of my older brother for too long.

To take my mind off it, I try to think about the up-coming Ceremony. I picture in my mind how our guests will look as they walk into the chamber and along the catwalk. They will be full of fear and elegance. Their eyes will gravitate to the inclined table, and the restraints, and the tubing which will funnel away the next victim's life blood. It's human nature to stare even though they'll do their damndest not to.

There's a new twist this time. It's been decided our fledging Detroit satellite will decide the identity of our victim.

I don't want to think that it will be Ruth. I know this isn't grief for her because I'm not capable of those kinds of feelings. Adam and I are like machines and we were born that way. No, it's more a regret because I am certain our new recruit in Detroit will choose the weakest for the Ceremony. If Ruth survives the vote it will be a miracle.

Chapter Twenty-one

Marty and Kal's old kung fu training centre lay in a quiet suburban street. Marty let herself in, got changed and then gave the punch bag all she'd got.

The reverb bounced off the brick walls. Sweat trickled down her back and she timed her strikes with her breaths, using her abdominal muscles to drive them home.

'Getting something out of your system?'

Marty glanced up. My god, it looked like Kal hadn't slept in over a week. That was dedication for you. Marty brought her concentration straight back to the bag.

Pam, pam.

The morning at Clarence had been dire. News of Sadie's death had fallen like a hammer blow on the team. Another death, and this time of a new staff member – it had knocked the stuffing right out of them. They'd each crawled off to their own corners. Frank and McIntyre were uncommunicative and sullen. Ian Taylor had taken to pounding the streets, and Miss Pringle had shut herself in the counselling room.

Marty exchanged punches for kicks. Meanwhile, Kal had disappeared into the changing rooms. Good, thought Marty, then they could get down to some kung fu combat, which was just what Marty needed.

Dressed in her training clothes, Kal waited while her friend finished beating the bag to death. It looked like the pressure of being at Clarence was starting to get to Marty. This type of work took a lot out of you.

They walked to the middle and bowed to each other. The two of them were regular combat training partners, or they had been. Kal didn't bother to ask Marty any questions yet.

Marty's feet danced on the mat. She was always so light and quick. Their old trainer said it was one of the skills of a great fighter. They exchanged a rapid series of strikes and Kal worked hard to counter each of Marty's moves until she found herself, *thunk*, flung onto the mat. Staring up at Marty, a glossy vein pulsing in her friend's neck, Kal waited for Marty to allow her to get up.

'It's been like hell at Clarence. The team are in pieces.'

Kal gave a grunt of acknowledgment as she rolled to her feet. She was careful to keep her eyes on Marty. She couldn't risk a blip in concentration, or, wound up like this, Marty would annihilate her. Marty steamed in again, getting in a couple of kicks to Kal's kidney area. They circled and exchanged strikes and then Kal found herself slammed onto her back for a second time.

'I found Beatrice practically catatonic.' Marty was breathless.

'She was sitting like a zombie, staring into space. She told me she wanted to go home only she was too scared. The poor woman was terrified someone might follow her.'

Kal got to her feet and moved out of reach and she ignored the pain in her knee. The injury she sustained in India was still a problem. She doubted it would ever heal properly and it meant she was no longer a real match for Marty. The days of them competing side by side in the National Championships were over.

'Right. It sounds like she's taken it really hard.'

'I felt so sorry for her. She was sweating, her legs were shaking. I had to practically carry her.'

'You looked after her.'

Marty looked at her friend, really looked at her, for the first time since she'd entered the room.

'Of course I did. I took her home. I checked all her windows and doors.'

Marty bounced on her toes, out of Kal's way.

'I toured the house a couple of times and reassured her again and again there was no one already there, lying in wait for her. It was not fun.'

'I know it wasn't. She trusted you and Beatrice was in good hands. In fact, probably some of the best.'

For a moment, she wondered if Marty might burst into tears, which would have been okay too, and very normal. Instead, Marty started pacing backwards and forwards.

'Thanks for coming. Hope I didn't give you too much of a beating. How's your knee holding up these days? It doesn't seem too bad.'

Kal didn't answer.

Marty retrieved her water bottle and splashed some onto her face. 'I really needed that. I feel much better.'

'Me too,' Kal lied, and she rubbed her sore back. 'And I'm going to take a shower. Listen, you said Beatrice was sensitive, so her reaction's in line with her temperament. Did she confide in you?'

'My god, you're hot on the shit, aren't you?'

Kal shrugged. 'It stands to reason. Beatrice was at a low ebb. She accepted your help, so the natural next step would be to confide or… confess.'

Marty didn't reply.

'Don't give me that look. That's the name of the game. We can't leave *anyone* out of the equation.'

'Yeah, I know. I wasn't prepared for the reality of it, you know – seeing trauma up close, suspecting everyone.'

'You'll get used to it. The aftermath and how people react is the precise time when all kinds of intelligence comes crawling out of the woodwork. Though we're not *suspecting*, we're keeping an open mind, until people prove themselves one way or another.'

Marty nodded. 'Frank and McIntyre closed in on themselves. Taylor went ballistic. Miss Pringle retreated and Beatrice cracked up. They all seem pretty normal reactions to me.'

They were heading for the changing rooms and Kal breathed in the welcome scent of soap. A hot shower would make her feel human again.

'She told me one thing which I think is going to turn out pretty important,' Marty said. 'The old centre manager was called Adam White. Turns out he was about to receive a formal warning and that's why he left.'

Kal stopped in her tracks. 'A warning for what?'

'Another member of staff saw him with a client. Adam and some girl were in a club and it was clearly a date and, of course, that's strictly against the rules. Beatrice said there'd been suspicions about him meeting clients socially before. The problem was they'd not got any evidence. She wouldn't tell me which member of staff reported it.'

'Right.'

'Adam White left over a year ago and he worked there for six years…'

Kal finished the sentence. '…so his employment falls in with the time-line of the killings.'

She clapped Marty on the shoulder.

'Great work, Marty, really great work. This Adam White needs some serious checking out. Things are starting to coalesce around the Clarence team. I've been talking to plenty of people on the street and rumours are pointing towards Clarence, not away.'

Marty had a terrible feeling Kal was right.

'Just remember to put your own safety first at all times, okay?' Kal said.

'As if I didn't know that already.'

Kal went on to tell Marty what she'd discovered about the local drug dealer, Samson. When the police released Samson from questioning, Kal had tailed him. He'd ended up at a night club and Kal had glammed herself up back at her old flat and then spent time dancing, then flirting and then sitting on Samson's knee. It had been worth it. She'd discovered Samson had

Inspector Taylor's mobile number in his contacts list. It was clear the two of them had regular discussions.

Marty gawped in admiration. How did Kal have the nerve to approach Samson let alone sit with him? Let alone use a window of a few seconds to check his phone?

'What next?' Marty asked.

'That's the million-dollar question. It seems to me we're missing the central, king pin. There's someone or something in the middle and these people are the satellites – Samson, Taylor and most likely Adam White.'

Kal kept her gaze away from Marty and spoke to the floor. 'That's why I wanted to meet. I say we head down to the coast. Something about Spinks' story doesn't add up.'

Chapter Twenty-two

The suburban streets sped past as Marty drove the two of them down to Brighton. Kal watched the urban landscape open up to reveal green fields and hedgerows and the Sussex countryside.

'This one will be up to you, Marty. You're going to take the lead.'

Marty tensed. This would be real responsibility.

'Amongst all the detail and the fluff and the garbage, there's going to be a slip of information about Sadie Tyler that will make a difference,' Kal said. 'There's a link somewhere, a connection, some common thread. Sadie was killed for a reason and you need to find out why.'

The words rang in Marty's ears as they headed for the social work office where Sadie had worked. Then, in the car park, without explanation, Kal abandoned Marty and headed off on a mission of her own.

Marty watched Kal go and she knew better than to ask questions. Kal would tell her the where and why when she was ready. Meanwhile, Marty had work to do.

Marty decided her strategy would be to opt for the truth, or at least, a partial version of it. She spoke to the woman at the reception desk.

'I know this is going to sound odd. I've come down from London and I wanted to meet Sadie Tyler's colleagues. I'm one of the workers from Clarence House and I know it seems strange for me visit at this terrible time and I know my manager has already passed on our condolences... I can't explain why I felt the need to come... I guess it sounds a bit lame.'

The woman examined Marty from head to foot. To Marty's astonishment, she accepted the explanation at face value. Which just shows what trusting souls social workers are, thought Marty. Just like I used to be.

'We got the news early today and we're all in shock, my dear. It's so dreadful. You'd better come and I'll introduce you to the others.'

The woman was so kind Marty felt a little guilty. The feeling grew as she was greeted as a welcome visitor and offered tea and biscuits and a sharing of the sympathy and horror.

Sadie had been part of a close-knit team. There were seven others clustered around a desk in the team leader's office. The team leader was a middle-aged woman, her hair tied back with a blue bandana and eyes that were red and swollen from crying. She explained they were in shock and she'd given them all leave to go home, though no one yet had, not wanting to break away from the collective support. Marty explained she'd come as an ambassador. At last the murmurings died down and someone collected their head enough to ask the obvious question.

'It's a long way for you to come, isn't it?'

'You're right and we didn't get to know Sadie yet, we were all ready to welcome her. In fact, that's why I came. I wanted to find out more about her. I suppose it's so I can tell the team back at Clarence.'

Her words opened a flood gate. Everyone had an anecdote to share – a memory of how they first met Sadie, a recollection of how caring she was, a snippet of how astute she was as a social worker. Marty learned Sadie broke up with her boyfriend and it had been hard, especially because he worked in the same building, though on a different floor and in a different team.

Marty tried not to drown under the details. Her mind worked frantically to collect the information, and, all the time, she sifted and searched for that golden nugget they were looking for. Nothing seemed to stand out. It all seemed very usual – Sadie was a nice person who'd led a dedicated professional life and had close workmates and friends. In her personal life, she'd had the highs and lows of any woman.

'Clarence House was going to be a fresh start,' one man said, echoing previous comments about Sadie's unhappy relationship break-up. 'You hear good things and bad things about London, don't you? She didn't really want to leave this place and when she found out Clarence was Adam's old workplace it made the decision a bit harder, which I could understand. But it was a dream job.'

In her excitement, Marty had to work hard not to shout. 'You knew Adam White?'

'Well, he was called Adam Mitchell when I knew him, and yes, me, Sadie and Adam did our social work

139

training together. Sadie really liked the role of the new job but when she realised Adam had been the manager there, it made her wobbly about making the move. Goodness knows why he changed his name. In fact, she only found out by chance he'd worked there when she saw him in a photo on their website. Anyway, she decided to ignore his involvement, given he'd left and all.'

'I didn't meet Adam,' Marty said. 'Were he and Sadie close?'

'No. It was a pretty intensive three years of training we did up at Sussex University. As I recall, one of her friends had a connection to him that went a bit wrong. But I don't know the details.' He turned away to close off the thread of conversation and it was clearly an avenue he didn't want to discuss further.

A short while later she politely excused herself and thanked them for their welcome.

Out in the car park, Marty paced around her car. This was the nugget and she couldn't wait to pursue it.

To her irritation, Kal wasn't answering her phone and Marty couldn't stand it. She was on to something. Why not go to Sussex University and see what she could find out? Maybe track down one of Sadie's old teachers? Yes, that would be her next step. So this was what it felt like to be hot on the trail of an evil perpetrator. It felt like fire in her veins.

Chapter Twenty-three

When Adam returned he knew straight away.

He'd been visiting the new satellite Lodge. Expansion was on the menu and the future of The Lodge was looking bright.

Or it was, until he discovered Tom's mess up. Tom had covered his tracks well, only not well enough. It was clear to Adam Ruth had been taken out of her cell for an unsanctioned session.

This presented Adam with a dilemma. Should he inform the Grand Master of the transgression? The Grand Master had strict rules and the punishment would be severe. Or should he keep silent and protect Tom as he'd always done?

Adam had known from the beginning Tom wasn't up to the mark. Tom was different. He wasn't like Adam. The difference being he didn't enjoy the hard stuff. He disliked the real violence and the subjugation. No, what Tom enjoyed was watching. He preferred to admire. He enjoyed the beauty of their guests and that made him a good scout. Of course, Tom enjoyed instilling fear like the rest of them though he did not enjoy physical injury. In short, he was a misfit.

Over the years, Tom's behaviour would never have gone unnoticed without Adam's assistance. Adam had influence. He had the Grand Master's ear and it was a position of power he intended to keep.

Adam adjusted his robes. This had come at a good time. He could use it to his advantage.

What his little brother didn't realise was the balance of power was about to shift. The Grand Master was becoming frail and a new leader was waiting to seize control. Adam had no intention of going out with the current Grand Master. No, he intended to choose sides wisely and move in to be the new, right-hand man.

The new contender was vicious and as ruthless as the person they wanted to replace and it was time to position himself beside the challenger. Of course, not in any obvious way that might place him in danger from their current leader. He knew the icy cruelty that lay behind the Grand Master's mask. No, he must be clever. And what better way to create a distraction from his own duplicity than to throw in a decoy? Tom would be the perfect ploy.

Adam's smile in the mirror was cold. He threw up the black hood and walked out of the room.

***

'Are you certain?'

Adam was careful to never look the Grand Master in the eye. He'd learnt that lesson as a child. He nodded as he stared at the filthy carpet.

The Grand Master sat on a red chair like a throne. To the side of the room was the bath tub their leader used. The Grand Master liked to recline in the blood of their victims and Adam knew the full truth about that. Marks around the tub indicated spillage onto the carpet and the Grand Master liked it that way – filthy and uncleaned – a reminder of the power they held over life and death.

Adam was used to the stink. Even the upholstery of the throne was stained. This was how the Grand Master liked it and it was how Adam had always known it, ever since his first waking breath.

'You may speak.'

'There's no denying it.' Adam was on his knees and he was careful to keep perfectly still. 'Tom took Ruth for a private, unsanctioned session. A banquet, as far as I can make out.'

He could sense the fury. Adam wondered if this would be one of the many occasions the Grand Master let vent to a torrent of insane screaming and ranting. He braced himself. Up to a few years ago, those type of fits left even Adam shaking to his bones. But they were much less frequent these days – another sign of the Grand Master's decline.

The leader shifted on the chair and a fetid waft of air met Adam's nostrils.

'He must be dealt with. His weakness has gone on long enough. You know what to do.'

Between the sentences, he could hear the Grand Master's snatched breaths. It betrayed their leader's recent illness. Yet the Grand Master held onto power with an iron clutch. There was still danger here.

Adam nodded. Yes, the time for change was close but the new contender would have to be very careful. When this meeting was over, Adam must report back every word to his new ally to make sure he gained favour.

Adam felt nothing for the man he was about to kill. His whole life had been killing and torture and death. Tom was his younger brother in name alone and he'd never truly been part of The Lodge. In fact, Adam had never felt anything for Tom except contempt – not one shred of compassion, not one drop of brotherly emotion. Emotions had never been Adam's weakness – he was as clinical as a well-oiled machine.

The death sentence was simply another task to be carried out.

'I'll see to it straight away,' Adam said.

Chapter Twenty-four

Dougie put on his favourite blue waistcoat and his favourite shoes. They were the ones with the black band down the side and the thick, white laces. He chose them because today was a special day.

Lying had never been Dougie's strong point. Fortunately, Simon was busy helping another resident. So when Dougie took his camera and backpack and told Simon he was going to Clarence House to take more shots, Simon didn't notice anything different from normal.

Dougie tied his laces with a double knot and walked down the stairs.

It was a lovely, sunny day and Dougie went his familiar route to the bus stop. He waited for the red bus that would take him to Clarence House. Except today he would be going further.

Today was March fourteenth. Before he went to bed every night, Dougie had been checking to make sure he didn't miss it. When Ruth told him, she'd written March fourteenth down in his little book. He thumbed to the place with her handwriting so often, the corner of the page was wearing away.

Dougie hadn't wanted to circle the anniversary date on his calendar because he knew someone would notice.

It had to be a secret. No one must know because Ruth had made him promise. On March fourteenth two years ago Ruth's dream was going to come true.

Since it was one of the usual drivers, she gave Dougie a friendly greeting when he got on the bus. Taking his customary seat at the front by the window, Dougie watched the shops rush by.

Routine was very important and Dougie liked doing the same things every day. That's why today was making him anxious. He counted the number of streets they passed, making sure to clock off the landmarks so he didn't get it wrong.

On the way up the hill, a woman wearing a black dress got on and sat on the other side of the aisle. A man rang the bell and got off at the stop for Clarence House and Dougie twitched because that was his usual stop.

The bus carried on. He and Ruth had only gone there once and he hoped he'd not get lost. Just like he'd done last year, he wanted to celebrate the memory of Ruth by going back there on his own.

Dougie shifted on his seat. He was a bit afraid of getting lost. He didn't like to be lost – it was a horrible feeling. He waited a few more minutes until the bus passed a post office. To Dougie's relief, the woman in the black dress rang the bell for the next stop, which meant he didn't have to reach up to do it himself. The driver pulled into the bay and the two of them got off.

This neighbourhood looked different. He could smell Chinese food and he looked down to see the remains of someone's takeaway smashed into the pavement. Going around the mess, he was careful to keep his shoes clean. First, he passed an estate agents, then a couple of fashion stores, and then a few doors down, Dougie found what he'd come for. He breathed a sigh of relief. And he felt very pleased he'd been able to find it again, all on his own.

This was where Ruth had brought Dougie to show him where she was going to have her special audition. Dougie cricked his neck to look up to the second and third floors and he thought of Ruth singing her heart out and it all being golden and wonderful.

The ground floor was a shop and the window was full of gold and silver items. The glittery jewellery caught the sun light.

With her busking money, which Ruth told Dougie she'd saved up especially for him, Ruth had wanted to buy Dougie a present. Dougie had been so pleased and he remembered how they'd examined all the items before he made his choice. In the end, he'd chosen a dragonfly brooch dotted with glass jewels. Then they had gone inside to make the purchase. Ruth pinned the dragonfly onto his jumper and the jewels on it glittered like diamonds.

'This is for you, Dougie,' she said. 'For being a special friend and the only person I'm going to tell my secret.'

Dougie had already been wide eyed at the lovely gift. Now he listened with rapt attention.

'You know where I've got my usual patch for busking, down by the underground exit?'

Dougie nodded.

'There's been someone coming to listen to me every day – a smart-looking man with dark hair. He likes my music. He says I've got talent!'

The excitement made Ruth's eyes shine.

'He recorded one of my songs with his phone and he's got a friend in the music business. The friend liked it and he's offered me an audition and it's this evening. Right here. Imagine!' Ruth squeezed Dougie's hand. 'What do you call that if it isn't the most fantastic thing ever! It's my lucky break, I can feel it.'

Dougie put his hand in his pocket and held the precious dragon fly brooch. That was the last time he'd seen Ruth. Part of him hoped she'd made it big and that one day, if he didn't see her at Clarence House, he'd see her on television, playing on some famous show. That's why he liked watching television at the weekends, in case he spotted her. He'd told Simon one time and Simon had smiled and said "I hope so too".

Normally Dougie kept the dragonfly brooch under his pillow. He could creep his hand under and go to sleep with the gift safe in his hand.

'Hello, haven't I seen you here before?'

The voice took Dougie by surprise. He instantly felt guilty. In the glass of the window he saw the reflection of a face that looked familiar. Turning, he almost tripped over his own feet. He had to steady himself on the window ledge.

'I didn't mean to startle you.'

The voice was friendly except the eyes were not.

Dougie pressed back against the pane and hoped he wasn't in trouble. He really didn't want Simon to know he'd not told the truth. And he hadn't been doing any harm. There was nothing wrong with looking at things, was there?

'Don't look so worried. Is it the jewellery you like? Why don't you come inside and I can show you a few pieces?'

Dougie wondered how to respond. What he really wanted was to go home. Yet this person was asking questions that weren't really questions. They wanted him to agree. Maybe he should take a quick look, then perhaps he'd be able to leave. Or should he simply stand still as a silent refusal?

The person was holding open the door and calling to someone else.

'Samson give me a hand. Let's get him inside.'

Dougie took a step back. He didn't like being touched by people he didn't like. He felt his sleeves being grabbed and they forced him into the shop.

Chapter Twenty-five

Marty was on a high.

'And get this for relevant,' Marty said. 'Sadie's best friend at University was called Helen and they were roommates. Helen now works as an assistant on the social work training course and what she told me will make your hair stand on end.'

Kal was staring out the windscreen, stony-faced. She'd been in a dark mood ever since Marty picked her up. Marty had no idea what was eating at Kal, but whatever it was, it looked bad.

Marty turned onto the motorway heading back to London. 'Are you listening or what?'

Marty had gone straight to Sussex University on the outskirts of Brighton. A campus site, Sussex University was set amongst the green, rolling hills of the South Downs, less than half an hour from Brighton town centre.

News of Sadie's murder had travelled fast. Once they made the connection between Marty, Sadie and Clarence House, everyone in the social work department had bent over backwards to welcome her. Marty had first spoken to a very helpful faculty secretary, then Sadie's old personal tutor, and finally Sadie's old roommate, Helen.

'I said, are you listening? This is important.'

'Shoot Marty, I'm all ears. Let's cut straight to the chase.'

'Okay, here's the short version – Sadie's roommate, Helen, had some very interesting stuff to tell. It turns out Helen and Adam were an item for a while. He was one hell of a weird character, though she didn't realise at first. Helen told me he acted like a regular guy. In fact, he was a bit of a smooth talker. Thing was, after the relationship got going, he wanted her to do strange things, kinky sex and stuff. Helen went along with it for a while. Then he introduced his younger brother, a guy called Tom, who wanted to watch them at it. That freaked her out and she doesn't know why, but she went along with it too, at least for a bit. Then Adam started getting edgy about her going out. He wanted to keep her inside. She said it got worse gradually until it was extreme. At one time, he even chained her to the bed in his apartment and left her there for *two days*. She got really scared and thought she would die of dehydration. After, she broke it off and she said she felt an utter fool for letting it go so far. Then, which was what she'd always suspected would happen, Adam wouldn't let her go. He started stalking her and Helen suddenly realised she'd always been afraid of him. In the end, Sadie persuaded her to go to the police. And this is the weirdest part…'

Kal gave Marty such a look, Marty almost swerved the car.

'Adam was exhibiting the traits of a psychopath,' Kal said. 'Someone who can carry the semblance of a

151

normal shell but it's simply an act. Then they set their sights on someone, usually a woman. The charm is the bait because it attracts the victim. And it's all deliberate because the predator is incapable of feeling any empathy. The woman starts to feel like they need to play along or it's going to get nasty, just like Helen did. The victim doesn't realise it's going to get even worse.'

'Er, sounds about right.'

'Carry on,' Kal said, dead-pan.

She'd known Kal for years, yet Marty's heart started beating fast. 'Yeah well, what I was going to say, and you're never going to believe this, the name of the police officer who interviewed Helen, was Detective Constable-'

'-Spinks.'

They both said it at the same time. There was a sudden silence in the car and Marty didn't feel like speaking another word. She couldn't tell if Kal was furious or upset, or both.

'Are you going to cut me in on what the hell is going on?' Marty finally said.

'I wish I knew and I'm sure as hell going to find out. While you were doing an excellent job questioning Sadie's old contacts, I followed up on a hunch. I'd already discovered Spinks did his initial police training in Brighton. Digging around a bit I found out his connection with the Adam Mitchell case.'

Marty risked a glance at her friend.

'Spinks never bothered to tell me he had history with Adam Mitchell or White or whatever he wants to call himself. It makes me think he didn't send Jennifer in simply because of the links between the missing women and Clarence, it was because he already had history with Mitchell-White. What the hell happened between them all those years ago? I know he didn't want me to come down to Brighton. Spinks tried to steer me away from Sadie's past.'

'Shit.'

And they were certainly up to their necks in it. Marty didn't want to state the obvious – that this dragged Spinks into the picture. She could see how Kal had taken that news very hard, after all, it had been belief in Spinks and working for victims that had saved Kal from going under since she discovered the truth about her own father.

Marty kept her eyes on the road and tried not to over-grip the steering wheel. What this meant was they were out on a limb. And well and truly on their own.

Chapter Twenty-six

When Ruth finally came back, she'd removed her make-up and nail varnish. She'd showered under the supervision of her masked tormentor, so all traces of perfume and luxury foods were washed down the plug hole. She again wore her baggy top and pyjama trousers. Ruth's bare feet dragged along the ground.

Delilah stared. Ruth was like a paper doll, so thin and fragile. Delilah could see Ruth's hair had been washed, though its sleek shine was a horrible contrast to the woman's emotionally ragged state. Ruth's eyes were the worst. Being forced to go with the mask and having to play along with its games had destroyed Ruth from the inside out. Seeing the pain in her friend cut Delilah like a knife.

Kirsten was cooing and shushing, trying to console Ruth and Delilah felt her heart breaking. They were useless. Helpless. There was nothing they could do for Ruth. And Kirsten might as well save her energy because Ruth wasn't responding. Was she even listening? It was as if Ruth had been swallowed whole by a black pit of despair.

Kirsten kept trying and it was so touching it filtered through to whoever Delilah had been before she came here. Something awakened. Sitting there helpless and hopeless, pressed against the bars as close to her two new friends as she could, Delilah had a sudden knowing. It was a sudden recall that told her she wasn't someone who gave up. She was a fighter. And as the newest one here, she had to use her strength while she still had it. It was her responsibility to help them all.

'This can't continue.'

Her words cut across Kirsten. The other two women were startled.

'We've got to get out of here. We've got to escape.'

'There's no way,' Kirsten said. 'If you try anything they'll half beat you or stun you to death.'

'I'd rather die than…' Delilah let it trail off and the unspoken horrors hung between them – rape, torture, humiliation.

'It's impossible. Don't you think we'd have tried?' Kirsten said. 'They're a bunch of sadistic killers. All in tune with each other like they've been brainwashed by fucking Satan. We don't stand a chance.'

'Satan doesn't exist. There's a person behind all this. A lunatic, yeah, I realise that. And maybe we don't have a hope in hell,' Delilah said. 'But we've got to try.'

Kirsten was shaking her head. 'We can't.'

'Listen to me, we've got to.'

'I didn't tell you,' Kirsten said. 'There was a woman in your cell before you came. Her name was Melissa and she was here when I arrived. Her hair was falling out in fistfuls. Let me tell you something else – do you want to know the reason Ruth started losing it?'

A woman in this cell before her? The notion hadn't occurred to her.

Kirsten was gripping the bars of her cell and the whites of her eyes were huge. 'Do you want to know what happened to Melissa! She was taken away for the *Ceremony*!' Kirsten was practically screaming. 'Afterwards, Ruth was taken and she had to mop up buckets and buckets of *blood*. Melissa's blood!'

'B-blood?'

'One horrific day you'll see for yourself. There's a sick, sadist ceremony. Worse than torture and being watched naked doing it with their fucking friends. In the ceremony, there's a fucking table rigged up with *tubes*. They tie you up and you *bleed to death*. Ever so slowly, while they watch. Something went wrong and there was a leak and Melissa's blood didn't get channelled away. Poor Ruth had to clean it up. A pool of it was covering the floor. Ruth knew what they were making her do and she had to shut the fuck up and do it.'

Delilah's mind had gone numb. She refused to believe it.

'I didn't believe it either when I was told about the ceremony. But it's the truth. We'll never get out of here alive.'

Delilah couldn't take it in.

'You're telling me one of us is going to be sacri-'

'That's why I didn't want to tell you,' Kirsten said. 'It's better not to know.'

It was beyond words. Delilah was stunned to silence.

'Like I told you,' Kirsten said. 'It's about survival. That's all we can do.'

156

Her head was spinning. Survive, but for how long? Until it was her turn to be taken to be raped? Until it was her turn to be taken to the table? Was that all she had left?

She sank to the floor.

Ruth was staring at her like a mad woman.

There was a long silence.

'How long have you both been here?' Delilah finally asked.

'I'm figuring I've been here more than a year. I used to keep count of my periods, until they stopped. Ruth, she's been here much longer than me.'

A scream began building in Delilah's throat. 'Oh god! I've got to get out.'

'Hey, it's all right Delilah. Everything's going to be okay.'

Kirsten was trying to console her in the same way she'd consoled Ruth minutes earlier.

'No it fucking well isn't!' Delilah dug her fingernails into her palms. She hoped she'd make herself bleed. 'I mean it Kirsten. I'm getting out and you can either help me or you can clear out of my way. Make your choice.'

This time the silence stretched out. Delilah felt a huge wave of exhaustion rolling over her. She gave up and went to curl in a ball on her bed. Her vision was going blurry again and she felt light-headed. Curse those bloody drugs, they were turning her into a vegetable. She must stop eating. It would make her weak it was true. It should also make her mind more focused. That's what she'd need if she was going to find a way out. Right, so no food from now on, or only tiny amounts.

When Kirsten spoke, Delilah jumped, her eyes suddenly wide open and staring into the gloom.

'If you get out, will you take the record from the other women with you?'

'Oh god, thank you Kirsten, thank you.'

Delilah was on the verge of tears. With Kirsten helping she might have a chance.

'I need you to tell me everything you know about this place – routines, timings, the layout beyond this room. What it's all like. What *they* are like.'

'I can do that,' Kirsten said. 'There are five of them and I know their traits.'

Delilah's head was swirling. Then she remembered what Kirsten had said.

'What record are you talking about?'

'It's a very special piece of paper and I like to think of it as a legacy. It was handed down to me by Melissa and it's a kind of record of all the women who have been here. I've been adding to it,' Kirsten said. 'When my time came…'

Kirsten's voice broke. '… when my time came I was going to pass it to you.'

Now Delilah realised she was actually crying. And she didn't care.

'It's all right,' Kirsten said. 'I won't abandon you. Who knows, maybe we can come up with an idea?'

How brave these women must have been. Trying to hold each other up. Supporting each other. Doing their best to keep a shred of dignity. Only Delilah couldn't be like that, she didn't want to end up like Ruth and Kirsten, counting the days until they led her away. She didn't have that type of courage. No, she'd made her decision. She would escape or she would die in the effort. That's who *she* was. That would be her legacy.

Chapter Twenty-seven

Dougie had been locked inside a small room, with a bucket and a mattress that smelled of baby sick.

Slumping in the corner, he felt tired and hungry and scared. They'd taken away his backpack. They'd pushed him against the wall and asked questions in nasty voices and with their bad breath wafting in Dougie's face. When he'd closed his eyes, they'd slapped him and he'd cried. That's when they'd locked the door and told him to shut up.

Hunching on the mattress, Dougie stared up at a square of frosted glass. He felt sure it led to the outside and he wished he could see the sky. They'd wanted to know what he was doing here and he hadn't told them. He hadn't whispered a word about Ruth or this being her special place where her dreams would come true. Dougie felt proud of himself for that. He screwed up his face and closed his eyes and hoped that Simon would come and find him soon.

Chapter Twenty-eight

Trampling around the countryside wasn't Kal's preferred mode of operation. She swore when a branch slapped her in the face. A few steps later and she swore again as she stepped in a puddle and muddy water splashed onto her trousers. There were valid reasons she was a city girl, she thought drily.

No one had driven along this track in a while. A passing vehicle would have left tyre marks and broken off greenery. At the end of the track, the Mitchell family house appeared deserted. Still, she must be wary. Someone could have been coming and going on foot.

Kal crouched at the edge of the trees and made a visual inspection of the property. Faded curtains at the windows, cobwebs hanging in the recesses of the door and a pile of leaves collecting at the entrance – no one had been to Adam Mitchell's childhood home in a while.

As Kal toured the outside of the building, the only sign of life was a bird which flew startled from a tree.

It would take a major effort to kick down the front door. Instead, she chose a window at the side, where the paint had been worn off by the weather and the wood was exposed along the bottom edge. On the second impact of her boot, she felt it giving way. The gap allowed insertion of a screwdriver. Then the wood splintered completely, giving enough space for her to jimmy the latch.

Understand a habitat and you understand a person. The inside of an apartment, a car, a room, even the contents of a bag said a lot about the owner. This old, abandoned house had been the place in which Adam Mitchell had been formed. She wanted to know everything it could tell her.

Kal climbed in to the kitchen. The stink inside was horrible. Scatterings of mouse droppings or more likely of rats, littered the floor. That was strange. Old houses had a certain kind of dirt and neglect to them and this one went above and beyond the normal. She wrinkled her nose. It wasn't a rotting corpse smell, so what the hell was it?

Using the light on her phone, she systematically checked the cupboards. If there had been secrets in this house, Kal wanted to find them. She wanted to know what had happened in this place to create a man who would chain a young woman to a bed and leave her there. After all this time, would the house tell her anything?

Everywhere she found filth, and with it came the unpleasant smell. She examined every room carefully and there were no trapdoors, no signs of a concealed entrance or compartment, no strange scrapes on walls or doorways. If children or adults had been incarcerated or abused here, it had left no marks on the structure. What she was expecting to find, Kal didn't know, except she knew she expected to find *something*. A tiny

162

indication. A suggestion of a direction to go in. Work the method, she told herself, and keep looking. An answer is here somewhere.

The cupboard under the stairs had no nail marks or scratches that might indicate someone had been kept prisoner there. Checking the recesses of the small space, she detected no rotting floorboards, to indicate old spillage of any kind, for instance of urine or faeces.

She heard the patter of rodents scuttling away, as she checked room after room.

Kal was halfway along the upstairs landing when she froze. The sound of a car engine came from outside and then it cut to silent. Voices filtered through – male, more than one person, and the slamming of car doors. Despite herself, her heart started thumping. Crossing quickly to a window, Kal peered down into the yard.

'Sarge,' a voice called. 'A window's been forced at the side.'

'I suppose that wasn't completely unexpected,' she said to herself.

By the time Kal retraced her steps back down the stairs, she found herself face-to-face with an angry Detective Chief Inspector Spinks.

***

Underneath his veneer, Kal could see Spinks' fury. It rippled along his jaw and got absorbed at the base of his skull. He should be careful about that, she thought, it was the kind of habit that could lead to a lifetime of skull-crushing headaches.

A uniformed officer jumped forward and pinned her arms behind her. Kal gave no resistance, concentrating on Spinks and still clocking his face and the emotions racing through him.

'I told you to stay in London,' he snapped. 'What the hell are you doing here!'

'If you get this oaf off me, I'll tell you.'

Spinks nodded to the man holding her. 'Give us a few moments, John.'

His voice was brittle and clipped as he gave orders. 'Take Peterson and get started with a search of the downstairs, and check there are no more *intruders*.'

Spinks glared at Kal who was rubbing her wrists.

'There's nothing to find. I already looked.'

'I told you to leave the Brighton investigation to me.' His eyes bored into her. 'Goddamit Kal! I need you on the streets. We're running out of time to find Jennifer.'

Spinks ran his fingers through his grey hair. He looked like a man who hadn't slept, a man haunted by ghosts of the past, she thought.

'Are you going to tell me what happened or do you want me to guess?' she asked. 'I can't help you find your missing officer if you don't trust me.'

'I trusted you enough to ask for help, isn't that enough for you? What the hell are you expecting from me? Blood, sweat and tears!'

Spinks looked very much like a man on the edge and she wanted him to tell her why. If he was going to make this hard so be it, but she would really prefer not to go that route.

'At least I gave you an excuse to gain access. You wouldn't have been able to legally enter if I hadn't been here.'

Spinks didn't answer.

She indicated the stairs. 'Shall we?'

Kal pretty much knew what Spinks needed to tell her – that he'd been a junior officer in the Sussex force and then transferred to the metropolitan police in London. That as a rookie detective, he'd been responsible for interviewing a young woman called Helen. The same Helen who'd made a stalker complaint against Adam Mitchell. According to Sussex police records, Sadie's roommate had later retracted her statement and refused to press charges. Only Kal wanted to hear the details from Spinks. He'd been the one who questioned Helen and interrogated Mitchell. The question was, would Spinks be willing to tell her? And if not, why not?

At the top of the stairs, they entered the first bedroom.

'How the hell did you know about this place anyway?' Spinks asked.

It would be a big mistake to let him know she'd gone to confront him and when he wasn't there, she'd used the few seconds she had to read the memo left on his desk by one of his team. Probably best never to mention that.

'I have my sources.'

'Of course you have.' He gave her a hard look. 'If you must know, the history of this case is complicated.'

'Try me.'

They locked eyes. Neither of them flinched and, in those moments, something shifted in Spinks. Or was he simply putting together his story so it would sound genuine?

Spinks began inspecting the room. After a few moments he started telling her how, early in this case, he'd seen photographs of the Clarence House staff. He'd spotted the old centre manager and he'd realised Adam White, ex-manager of Clarence House, was one and the same as Adam Mitchell, the man who'd chained a young woman to a bed down in Brighton. It had been a nasty shock. Spinks told Kal that when he sent in Jennifer Morris, he could think of nothing except the man he let get away, all those years ago.

'I was young and I made a terrible error of judgement. I was inexperienced. I pushed that young woman hard because I wanted the conviction in court. But I went too far. I can see her face now, all scared and pale as a sheet. Helen was terrified of testifying in court, even if she had the witness screens to protect her from seeing Mitchell. He was an absolute animal. How the hell he ended up as a social worker I'll never know. I pushed and pushed that young woman to testify, and in the end, she couldn't go through with it. She withdrew her statement and it was my fault.'

Kal was leaning against the wall, watching Spinks.

'Adam Mitchell, who changed his name to White,' Spinks said, 'was a vicious man who'd terrified a young

166

woman and it was because of me he got away with it. The man was deranged.'

'Right. And you didn't think to mention this to me before?'

Spinks threw back a carpet which was so dirty, the pattern on it was impossible to make out. A cloud of dust filled the room and they both choked. When they'd recovered, Spinks began again.

'I thought about it and I dismissed the idea. I wanted to handle the Brighton side of things myself. That's why I told you to stay in London. I thought it would be best.'

Why was it something still didn't hang right? It was just too easy. No, there was a deeper layer to this. Spinks still hadn't told her the whole truth.

'Anything else?' she asked.

'Can we get on with the work? Isn't that what we're here to do?'

He was covering up, she knew it. Protecting himself, though not from exposure about failing with Adam Mitchell-White. No, she was pretty sure he'd not kept this a secret in order to protect his own reputation. So then what was he covering up? And why?

'What about Inspector Taylor?'

'What about him? I told you already, Ian is a good man.'

'A good man! You're kidding me, right? He followed you up from Brighton, didn't he? Was he involved in the Mitchell-White case too?'

Anger flickered across Spinks' face.

'You've really been checking up on me haven't you? I suppose I shouldn't have expected anything less.'

Spinks kicked the carpet to the side.

'Taylor transferred from Brighton to the London Metropolitan police the same time as me, yes. But he had zero involvement in the Mitchell-White case. For your information Taylor was still in training at that time.'

'Taylor is obsessed and unhinged and out of control.

'Did you get more evidence?'

Spinks and Taylor could be in this up to their necks. Maybe Spinks wanted to check what she had on them.

She shook her head.

'Ian's not involved, he can't be. I've no explanation for what you saw at his house and of course that's out of order only it's not a crime, it's a contravention of procedures. For the last couple of years Inspector Taylor has wanted to join the Criminal Investigation Department and unfortunately he's failed the detective's exam twice. If there's anything egging him on, it's his own frustrations. It's against protocol to take information from the crime files but-'

'Don't tell me. He's a good man.'

Spinks walked out and she followed him to the next bedroom.

Spinks was already lifting another filthy carpet. He tossed it to the side and she watched as he crouched to examine the floor boards for unusual wear and tear, at the same time trying to keep his own clothes from trailing in the dirt.

Kal's suspicions were like half-wild dogs refusing to heel and yanking at her attention. Yet she knew part of her wanted to let him off the hook. Catching killers wasn't all about being a machine – she realised that more and more. Strategy was important. Psychology was important. Her father had taught her all of that. But what he'd left out was how important it was to keep connections to good people. And this man in front of her was, or had been, one of the best. He'd already proved that in hunting for her mother and then in working with Kal to bring down a serial killer.

Deep down inside, Spinks was someone she wanted to think well of. And a little voice told her Spinks wasn't being totally open because he was protecting something personal. Nothing to do with his involvement. Nothing to do with covering up for Taylor. No, Spinks was protecting something personal to him and precious and that made her want to stand by him. Then again, what if she was kidding herself and her judgement was way off because she'd been weak enough to like him?

'Have you tracked down Adam yet?' she asked.

'He's dropped off the grid. I've got a whole team trying to trace any living relatives.'

They moved on to the last bedroom and Spinks said nothing more about Taylor nor Brighton, though she noticed how he toyed with the little eagle pin at his lapel.

There was the same stink and a thicker layer of grime on the floor in this room. Kal prodded at it with the toe of her shoe. Sludge rolled up like black toffee.

169

'All this dirt up here,' she said. 'Where the hell did it come from? And that smell. You don't suppose…'

They both had the same thought.

'I've some equipment in the back of the car,' Spinks said. 'We can check.'

When he came back a few minutes later, Spinks wore forensic gloves.

'A spray of luminol will show any blood stains,' he said. 'If there's even a trace, it's all we need. It will be enough to call in forensics.'

Kal nodded. Any blood stains would glow green-yellow from the luminol. It was a quick method and very efficient.

His arm swept in an arc, covering the floor and a portion of the wall. And what showed up was a green-yellow glow that covered the whole of the area he'd sprayed on the floor.

'My god, this layer,' Kal said. 'It's not filth and dirt.'

Spinks was already taking his phone out of his pocket.

There was something else. On the edge of the glowing stain, two tiny objects jutted out from between floorboards. She bent closer. They were two molar teeth, and human looking.

'Someone's jammed two teeth in the crack here.'

Spinks stopped what he was doing.

Kal kept staring at the teeth. Why would someone put them here? They were both lined up side by side and they weren't pointing to the ceiling, they were angled towards the wall. It didn't look like an accident, the way they were placed neatly beside each other. It looked as if someone had deliberately placed them there. In fact, both of them had been set at the same angle. With her eyes, she followed the line. They pointed to a patch on the wall.

'Spray more luminol here,' Kal said, and she pointed to the wall.

The chemical left no stain.

'There's been no blood there,' she said. 'Which is strange because I was expecting to see something.'

Spinks nodded.

Crouching down, Kal pointed to the section of skirting board at the base of the wall. It looked as if it might be slightly looser than the others.

With one gloved hand, Spinks prised off the section of board. It must have been removed at one time and pushed back because the nails didn't really hold it firmly. She heard him suck in a breath. They didn't need the luminol.

Behind the skirting board someone had written a message in blood.

"My name is Debbie Please Help me"

Chapter Twenty-nine

It was a relief to get out of the house and away from the stink and a filth that would probably turn out to be mostly dried blood. Whoever Debbie had been, she had certainly suffered in that room at the top of the house. The police would now take this place apart plank by plank. Her job here was done.

Despite the sunshine, Kal shivered. What would make someone so desperate? Someone would have to have been in that room for one hell of a long time to come up with the idea of dislodging two of their own teeth, let alone actually manage to work their own molars free. Had Debbie been there so long she suffered from malnutrition and her teeth loosened? Did it mean she'd been starved? And who was she?

Kal took a few deep gasps of air and tried to rid her clothes of the smell.

This was a very isolated spot. The house lay on the outskirts of a picturesque village called Ditchling. Here the Mitchells had been surrounded by Sussex countryside, with the rolling hills of the South Downs forming a long, natural barrier between them and the coastal town of Brighton. This was the kind of place where no one would hear your screams. At that thought, a shiver ran up her back.

Her phone buzzed and up came a response from Marty. Kal scanned the text. Fifty years ago, the daughter of a well-known Sussex artist had gone missing, and the daughter's name had been Deborah. Despite an extensive police search, Debbie had never been found. In newspaper articles from that time the girl was described as "an auburn-haired beauty". She was also a talented artist, just like her mother.

Things were starting to fall into place. In London, the victims were selected for their beauty, like Ivana and Ruth. Talent also played its part. And now here was a missing girl called Debbie who had been an artist. And she went missing fifty years ago.

As she sat on a tree stump thinking it through, something caught Kal's eye. It was an unnatural little flick in the corner of her vision.

Old leaves crunched underfoot as Kal walked towards the spot where she'd seen movement. Ahead of her, on the trunk of a huge tree, a black object had been pinned out.

It was a large black bird strung with its wings out. The feathers were worn, and many were missing and she could make out the fine bones in the wings. Judging from the state of it, it must have been here for years. Farmers did that kind of thing, didn't they? To scare away other birds. She'd read that somewhere. Only this was the woods. On the other hand, cults used objects like dead birds and pentagrams and signs in blood. At least, they did in films. But then this wasn't a horror film. Or was it?

By that logic, this was either an invitation or a warning to keep out. Kal pushed on into the trees.

This time she didn't care about being scratched by branches and getting slapped in the face. She had an image in her mind of an auburn-haired girl named Debbie, trapped and tortured by members of the Mitchell family.

She soon found what she was looking for. It was an old barn. Its stone construction suggested it was much older than the house. The wooden door was three-quarter sized and had a curved top and it hung off its hinges.

She entered the barn. Bats must have nested in the roof, because a trail of droppings ran down the wall and onto the floor.

Kal walked through the droppings and her eyes adjusted to the lower level of light. She saw stone flooring, no window, and an oblong slab sitting in the middle of the barn, about knee-high and large enough for a person to lie on. Kal ran her hand over the smooth, cold stone. A row of symbols had been carved along one end. She didn't recognise the script. But there was something very odd about the size of the slab and it was giving her goose bumps.

Kal walked slowly around the slab. The coroner had speculated the deaths by exsanguination of the London victims could be explained by a ritual sacrifice method. Until now, she'd been sceptical about that.

At the head of the slab she found two channels carved in the floor. They ran diagonally away from the top corners of the slab and out to the far corners of the barn. The floor had been designed on a slight incline so the channels ran downwards to the walls.

She'd have been very pleased, and relieved, if Spinks had chosen to make an entrance at that point. Kal was imagining Debbie tied down whilst a person or persons took away her life and whilst her blood ran red in the two channels.

Barbaric killings had taken place here. And someone, or a group of people, had transplanted the same practices to modern-day London.

If the blood was channelled away, why was so much of it showing up in the house? What did that say about the people behind this operation? That somebody relished smearing themselves in a victim's blood?

'You can wash away blood, but you can't wash away a body,' she said to herself.

Why would the perpetrators bother to go to the hard work of transporting bodies to bury them when they had all this woodland available on their doorstep? No, the killer or killers felt immune to discovery. And that would be their downfall. The police would blast this site with all the science and the resources they'd got and they'd find the evidence. The only problem being it would take time. And time was what Jennifer didn't have.

She tramped back to the house. Sacrifice. Ritual. A group of like-minded killers intent on their purpose. There would be a body here to find, she felt certain. Probably more than one.

There'd been instances of family collusion in serial killer cases. She'd read details of where a homicidal tendency had passed down to the next generation, and even of parent and son, or parent and daughter homicidal partnerships.

The village of Ditchling was a small, rural community and it must have been a law unto itself in the olden days. A little knot of cottages where people felt they could do what they liked. And why hadn't the police found the barn during their search for the artist's daughter fifty years ago? Had the local police been bribed. Or had they been part of it?

She imagined again a victim restrained on the stone slab, this time allowing herself to delve into the mind of the killers. Perhaps on-lookers observed, no, participated, in the ceremony. They moved as one. Maybe they wore special clothing. Would they be silent? Would they chant? Who would those participants be? Family members? Kal forced herself to imagine the worst. This mind must hold no fears for her, so that when she confronted it, she'd be ready.

Chapter Thirty

By the time Kal got back to London, it was late afternoon. In the last few hours, a whole battalion of experts and their equipment had descended on the Mitchell house. As Kal left, they were preparing to start the long search for human remains. The house would be taken apart. The ground would be dug up inch by inch and any findings painstakingly photographed and catalogued. The work could take months.

Someone had organised a massive sandwich delivery for the team and Kal had eaten two of them and taken two more to share with her friends. The sergeant who'd pinned her arms noticed her tucking them away and he'd laughed, telling her to take as many as she wanted – in fact, the whole team seemed to have been transformed into her best friends since her discovery of Debbie's message.

Kal walked along the Thames river. The light reflected from the water and she paused as a boat load of visitors made its way close to the river bank, the passengers snapping pictures as they went. She could make out the excited calls of the tourists.

Locating Adam and his family was now top of the police's list and Kal had been thinking through her own priorities. They were pulling the net around the perpetrators tighter but not tight enough and not fast enough. She must step it up. Time to put more pressure on her homeless contacts for a final push.

'Kal!'

She swivelled, the pavement greasy underneath her shoes. A figure ran along the path. At first a dark blob, as it came closer it transformed into Simon, though not the calm Simon she'd seen before. He looked exhausted and scared.

Kal didn't bother with pleasantries. 'What's wrong? What the hell's happened?'

Simon was out of breath. 'It's… Dougie.'

Kal's heart jumped into her throat.

'Tell me what happened!'

Simon rested his hands on his knees, his chest heaving. Kal had to restrain herself from grabbing his lapels and shaking more out of him. At last he straightened up.

'Dougie's missing. I'm so glad I bumped into you. Please tell me you've seen him.'

Oh god no, not sweet, innocent Dougie.

She shook her head and she saw how that one gesture washed away Simon's hopes. He was giving way to panic. Panic was a wild type of energy which blew holes in your brain and could make you run in circles. It wouldn't do Simon, nor Dougie, any good. She put a hand on Simon's shoulder and gestured for them to sit down.

'I can't, I've got to keep looking. He's been gone all day.'

Kal applied a little more force to her arm and Simon yielded.

'I want to help you find him. Only first you've got to tell me exactly what happened.'

Simon nodded and collapsed on a low wall. 'It'll be dark soon and Dougie's frightened of the dark.'

'I know,' she said, injecting a calm into her voice which she didn't feel. She needed to hear the details. It would help her pinpoint the important information. Help her focus on what would count and make a difference.

It turned out Dougie had set off for a normal morning of taking photographs outside Clarence. When Simon came to collect him at mid-day Dougie was nowhere to be seen. None of the staff had spotted him that day and the regular centre users hadn't noticed him.

Staff from the group home had searched Dougie's other favourite haunts – a photography gallery in the high street with a friendly manager, the comic book section of the library, the duck pond at the park, the places Ruth used to play music. When they'd come up with an absolute nothing the police had been alerted. Dougie was a vulnerable adult and the police had joined the search. So far, everyone had drawn a blank.

Kal's mind felt clear. Yet again in this case, there was no such thing as coincidence. There had to be a connection. Dougie had disappeared for a reason. Which likely meant someone must think Dougie knows something. Something to do with Ruth's disappearance? A key fact linking together the missing

179

young women? Or worst of all, had someone followed her trail and it led them to Dougie?

'Was there anything different about Dougie this morning? Did you notice any changes in his routine or how he seemed in himself?'

'I wish I had,' Simon said. 'If anything, he'd been more cheerful lately. I think it might have been after meeting you.'

Kal stared. 'What?'

'I'm not being funny. Like I said to you before, it's because you remind him of Ruth, I mean, in a good way, because you're actually here in the flesh and blood.'

The thought she might have led to Dougie being in danger made Kal see red. A memory replayed of the exchange she'd witnessed between Dougie and Frank with Frank leaning into Dougie and towering over him. It lit the fuse on her temper and she knew exactly what she would do next.

Chapter Thirty-one

Sometimes it's wise to do things on your own. At other times, it's better to have back up at hand and this was one of those instances when going it on her own would be foolish.

Bringing in Marty was out of the question. With her high standards of right and wrong, Marty would never condone what Kal was about to do. In fact, if Marty never heard about this, it would be all the better.

Kal thumbed through the contacts on her phone and selected LeeMing's number. He answered quickly and after a short conversation she hung up.

That was the good thing about knowing people like LeeMing. LeeMing knew the score. He was always there for his friends, and Kal felt herself lucky to be counted as one of them.

It hadn't been like that at the beginning. LeeMing was the new lead trainer at the kung fu club, taking over from their old trainer who'd retired. Against the odds, LeeMing became a firm friend during Kal's investigation into the disappearance of her mother. He'd been key in holding it all together, and later he'd helped Marty when she was fighting for the life of a young boy. LeeMing had special skills because, for years, he'd been an active member of the Chinese mafia, known as the Triad.

Now he walked a straight and narrow line the correct side of the law. He was the right person to call in for her clandestine operations because he lived by his own code, which was much more flexible than Marty's. Besides, she only really wanted LeeMing as look-out. She would be the one getting her hands dirty.

It was a crisp evening and there were plenty of people on the streets, rushing this way and that like insects, as they always seemed to do in the metropolis. Everyone was always on the move, forever busy. Right by her elbow, a young couple started kissing, totally oblivious to her presence. She could swear she could hear the slurp of their lips.

From the street corner, Kal watched the entrance to Clarence House until she saw Miss Pringle leaving. The counsellor hurried to the bus stop with her hands in her pockets and her eyes down. Hardly the right attitude or posture to avoid problems on the street, thought Kal.

Kal flexed her shoulders and rubbed her hands together. No one had yet glanced her way, but this position was too exposed. She sank deeper into her own hood and made sure her hair was tucked out of sight. The last thing she wanted was to attract attention.

The couple were still stuck to each other's faces, as next out of Clarence came Marty. She walked fast with a swinging stride and her head held high and Kal couldn't help smiling. How lucky she was the two of them had been thrown together all those years ago.

Next out were Frank and McIntyre. The two of them walking together might cause a tiny complication. She'd have to see how this one panned out.

Keeping back as far as she dared, Kal crossed the road and fell into step behind them, blending with the other pedestrians.

At the end of the road, they parted and Frank peeled off to the right. Kal kept her emotions steady. This wasn't the time to indulge excitement or anticipation, this was work she must get exactly right. She had no doubt that more than one life depended on it, including Dougie's.

It still amazed Kal how easy it was to take someone by surprise. Most people were so wrapped up in their own thoughts and preoccupations, they noticed little of what was happening around them, right here and now. Frank was no exception.

Of course, Kal's great advantage was her mastery of Dim-mak – the ancient art of using pressure points to inflict serious injury, or even death. On this occasion, she tailored her use of force to a lower notch, coming up behind Frank and putting her hand on his neck to locate the pressure point. Frank was startled. Then when he saw it was a woman, his unconscious let him drop his guard. He didn't see her as much of a physical threat.

By the time she was applying pressure he was too slow to react. With Dim-mak, size really didn't matter and she subdued Frank within a few seconds. The big man slumped to a heap.

Frank was bloody heavy and she needed to get him out of sight before some good Samaritan passer-by rushed to help her, thinking he was ill or something. On cue, LeeMing appeared, pulling the van up smoothly at the kerbside. The two of them hefted Frank into the back and they drove off.

Kal tossed back her hood and unzipped her jacket. 'Did you get the merchandise?'

LeeMing raised an eyebrow.

'I'm not handing it over until you tell me to my face what this,' LeeMing jerked his head towards Frank in the back, 'is about.'

She filled him in on the case and then repeated what she'd told him on the phone, knowing that it wasn't he didn't trust her, he wouldn't be here if he didn't. No, LeeMing needed to make sure this sat properly with his conscience and how she told it in the flesh was different to hearing it down a mobile phone. She told him about Jennifer and Dougie and Marty at Clarence House undercover, the discovery of Debbie's desperate message and her own suspicions about the perpetrators.

LeeMing listened to the whole package. At the end, he nodded his agreement.

***

Frank had a nice place.

Kal locked the front door behind them. It had gone without a hitch. She'd researched where Frank lived and his most likely route home. That was rudimentary. She also knew there were no CCTV cameras on the stretch she grabbed him, so they wouldn't have been caught on footage. And they'd taken him when the street lay deserted. Perfect. Her father would have been proud of her.

LeeMing handed her a small package. Kal ripped it open, rolled up Frank's sleeve and jabbed the needle in his arm.

Ten minutes later, they had Frank blindfolded and strapped to one of his own dining room chairs. Kal waited for him to come round. Frank wouldn't realise they'd pumped him full of a mind-altering drug. It would loosen him up and speed up the questioning process.

Kal paced the living room. Simon has sent her a message telling her there was no news and he was staying out all night searching the same places over and over again. When she read it, fury overtook her.

She warmed up her shoulders and back.

As Frank gave a groan, LeeMing moved to the side. He said only one thing to Kal.

'Don't go too far.'

Smack.

Before he could work out what was going on, Kal cuffed Frank on the side of the head. She followed it up with a full-force double punch to the gut. Frank caved and gave a shout of fear and confusion. There was anger in his voice too and that wasn't good. Probably it came from his size and strength. And it caused a problem because an angry person would never be compliant. Kal wound back for another strike. Frank wasn't easily intimidated. She knew he wouldn't talk until that defiance was out of him.

Smack.

Roughing people up really wasn't her style. But needs must.

'I'm going to ask some questions and you're going to give me proper answers,' she said.

Frank laughed. 'Like hell I am.'

She gave him another double whammy to the gut. The sound of her fists reverberated off the walls.

LeeMing had gone into the kitchen next door. She could hear him running water at the sink so she took the opportunity and gave Frank a few more doubles. The thought of Dougie alone and frightened helped her keep her resolve.

Her knuckles were stinging and Frank's torso was colouring up. A trail of clear liquid ran from one of his nostrils and she could hear his breathing getting heavier.

Come on Frank, don't make this harder than it has to be.

'Like I said, I've got some questions I want answering.'

Frank spat on the floor and she saw blood in his saliva. It wasn't the bright red blood that would spell danger. No, it came from the inside of his mouth. His teeth must have caught his cheek.

'Okay, whatever the hell you want,' he said. 'Now take off this bloody blindfold. Who the hell are you?'

His anger had dissolved. Now he was trying to work out what was going on. He was trying to manoeuvre to get information which might help him. Good for Frank. At least it showed he wanted to get himself out of the vulnerable position he was in.

'Shut up!' She paced in front of him. 'Question one – where the hell is Dougie?'

'I don't know anything about Dougie. How the fuck would I know where he is!'

She really lost it then and it wasn't until LeeMing put his hand on her arm that she reined herself back. By then, a trickle of blood ran down the side of Frank's face.

Kal started pacing again. Her own breathing was ragged.

'Answer the fucking questions fucker!'

It came out as half scream and before she knew it she was right on top of him. This time she was brandishing a pair of scissors she'd grabbed from Frank's desk. She dragged the tip of the metal down his cheek.

Kal made her voice go icy like her father's. 'There's a lot of damage you can do with a pair of scissors. Did you know that?'

Frank said nothing.

'Now hold very still.'

Grabbing Frank's head, she inserted the sharp end into his ear. He didn't know what the hell was going on and was too worried to try to jerk his head away. David Khan's murderous nature had taught her a lot.

Now Frank froze. He would feel the scissors cold and metallic sliding into his ear channel. He wouldn't be able to stop his instincts screaming "Danger!".

'You're a fucking madwoman.' His voice was tight as he tried to talk without moving his head one iota.

'That's right, I am.'

She pushed the scissors in a little further and watched with satisfaction as Frank broke out in a cold sweat. Terror really was an amazing reaction.

'Now shall we have our little chat again?' she said in a sing-song voice. 'Be careful now, don't move your head.'

LeeMing coughed. He'd asked to be kept out of it but he made the noise deliberately, she thought, to let Frank know there was more than one person in the room. Or perhaps it was to remind her that he was right there, watching everything she did, ready to step in and pull her back if he needed to.

'Now tell me where I can find Dougie,' she said, dead-pan.

'I don't know where he is, I swear it.'

'I saw you outside Clarence. You threatened him.'

'I never did! I talked to him, that's all. He comes all the time to check on the girl he liked. I gave him chocolate. I'd never hurt someone like him.'

Kal twisted the scissors a little. Not being able to see Frank's eyes put her at a disadvantage as far as judging lies from the truth. But from the amount of sweat rolling down Frank's neck, he'd have to have one hell of a load of balls to lie in this situation. If she pushed the scissors in not very much further he'd be deaf for life on that side and if she pushed further still into his brain, he'd be dead.

'You know don't you Frank, that right the other side of your fragile little ear drum is your brain? With the angle of the ear canal, it's a bit tricky to know what I'll hit when I pierce through. I'm hoping for the brain stem but then again, the cerebellum wouldn't be a bad target.'

'It's the truth. I swear I haven't touched Dougie. I don't know where he is!'

Frank was slurring his words. That was a positive sign because it meant LeeMing's drugs were effective. Yes, very likely he was telling the truth.

The heat suddenly went out of her and Kal carefully withdrew the scissors. Now she was all cool strategy.

'Tell me about the missing girls. And the dead ones.'

'I don't know anything. I'm not some kind of fucking pervert! You've got the wrong man.'

Frank's inflection when he said "fucking pervert" had the right ring to it. Even in this situation, most serial killers would have given a sly reply. They liked to show off and out-smart others, to twist and weasel their way. To toy with their interrogators as part of the game. To give a little hint and at the same time get people running in circles. And what about a little knot of killers? What was their behaviour under pressure? That was more of an unknown. But now it didn't seem to her Frank was part of that gang.

'Tell me about Adam White and don't fuck me around if you don't want to be brain-dead.'

'There's nothing to tell. I did the right thing.'

'Explain.'

'I snitched on him. It's not something I'm proud of.'

'What the hell is that supposed to mean? You're stretching my patience Frank.'

'I'm trying to cooperate! I saw Adam dating one of the users of Clarence House in a club. Adam tried to blackmail me to keep quiet because he knew I'd got a girl pregnant and she was a client at Clarence House too. She wasn't under age, I swear it. He told me if I told, he'd tell on me and I'd be sacked for it. That it would be me who'd be kicked out, not him.'

'And?'

'I went ahead and told the committee about Adam anyway. Of course, it meant he told them about me but in the end, Adam was asked to leave and I got disciplined.'

'Lucky bastard aren't you,' she said, whispering in his ear, the one she'd just threatened. Frank winced.

'What the hell do you want!'

Kal was sorely tempted to kick him in the balls for sleeping with that client only she didn't. Frank didn't have the answers she wanted and no amount of force was going to fabricate them out of him.

'What do I want? I want my friend back you ass-hole. And if I find out you had anything to do with it, I'll be coming back to hunt you down.'

Chapter Thirty-two

The fragile sheets of paper had been carefully preserved and passed from woman to woman. Where the originals came from, Kirsten had no idea, nor the pencil, nor who had first thought of rolling it around the pencil and then pushing the package into the piping running along the wall of the cell. In that way, it had remained undetected by their captors.

Kirsten knew when it was safe to talk because her cell was the only one with a grille leading to a ventilation shaft. When no one else was in the house, Kirsten could guess it by the lack of vibration and the absence of slight noises that otherwise drifted to her from the floors above.

The house was quiet again and Kirsten stood on her bed and felt inside the piping. With her finger, she pulled the paper towards her, feeling it slide along the plastic. As the end came into sight, she pulled the little roll free, careful not to rip the fraying edge.

The sheets were covered with tiny writing. Each woman had left a message and signed her name. By the time it came to the end, most everyone had remembered their real name, though the majority chose to share it only with the paper and not with their cell-mates.

Kirsten felt a sudden urge to kiss the yellowing page, as if it were a holy parchment. In a way, she supposed it was. It was a witness statement of all the lives that had been tormented and then been lost.

She already knew the whole of it by heart. Delilah would have to learn it. If she ever made it out, she'd take the legacy of the other women with her.

Kirsten rewound the paper round the pencil. Reaching as far as she could, she handed it through the bars. Delilah, arm outstretched to the limit, grasped it with her fingertips. She had to crunch the end slightly to grab it and it was all Kirsten could do to stop herself shouting out in rage. Yes, Ruth wasn't the only one who was losing it, she thought to herself.

Delilah took the paper to her bed to inspect it. Instinctively, Kirsten knew they'd not be hearing from Delilah for a long while. When Kirsten had first read it herself, she'd cried for days. Yet she realised Delilah was different. To her, it would do the opposite, it would put a fire in her. Make her even more determined than she was already.

There was one thing Kirsten hadn't said and she wasn't going to. She'd not told Delilah she felt sure it was a choice between herself and Ruth for the next ceremony. Which meant they should both put their names on the paper before it was too late.

The night before, Kirsten had added her name and her message. Only she didn't want to remind Ruth to, because it was like asking someone to sign their own death warrant.

Kirsten thought back to the beginning to when Ruth had saved her, because when Kirsten first arrived, Ruth's gentle singing had kept the demons from devouring Kirsten whole.

Ruth was her true friend. Captivity meant they knew each other down to their souls. Yet, in her most secret thoughts, Kirsten hoped it would be Ruth they'd pick and not her. And that thought was like acid. It made her hate herself. This place had made an animal of her. It had made her into a monster just as bad as them and that's why Kirsten determined to help Delilah escape – so she'd never have to face the same soul-destroying thought herself.

***

The way Kirsten handled the paper, you'd think it was sacrosanct, thought Delilah. In fact, once she had it, Delilah realised how flimsy it was. The sheets were falling apart. The writing was so faded, she had trouble reading it. She'd memorise what she could, to the best of her ability, out of respect for the other women. She owed them that.

Who would be taken away next? And for what? When would be the next ceremony? The not-knowing and the constant terror wore away her stamina and her strength, like water rubbing away soap. Delilah feared she was getting whittled down to nothing.

Delilah was eating as little as she dared. At times, she'd started feeling light-headed not from the drugs but from starvation.

Kirsten had an idea and together they'd made a plan. She *must* hold out until the next ceremony. Delilah didn't want to think too hard about what little chance they'd have. If she thought like that she'd curl up in a ball and wait out the long and horrible years. And have to perform on the harp her Welsh grandmother had taught her to play and do whatever depraved sex acts they ordered for their gratification. No, she refused.

When she had her small chance she'd take it. The next ceremony would be her opportunity.

Then again, was she prepared to leave the others behind to their fate? Delilah didn't want to think about that either. She was escaping to save them, not to abandon them. If she could get out, she'd be able to bring help. Kirsten and Ruth could live. Delilah took a deep breath and pushed all the doubts away.

Sitting on the floor of her cell, once again, she tried to concentrate. Delilah began memorising the contents of the paper.

Chapter Thirty-three

When Kal jogged up the path, Marty stopped her warm up exercises.

'You decided to ditch the homeless image then?' Marty said.

'Yes, I got what I wanted and it was well worth it. The street sleepers came out great. I don't have much time so I thought we could catch up on a quick run across the Common.'

Now that Marty looked more carefully, she could see a familiar glint in her friend's eye. It was the same manic gleam which, throughout Kal's childhood, always got her into trouble. The look that invited fights and conflicts. Back then, it had been Marty who'd rescued Kal and when necessary, dragged her away by the scruff of her neck.

Marty fell into step beside her friend. That look in her eye meant Kal was going wild and a bit reckless. It was the dangerous side to her friend's brilliance. Damn, LeeMing had been right. He'd warned Marty to try to keep Kal close.

They took the trail across Wimbledon Common, matching each other stride for stride.

'Any progress on tracing Dougie?' Marty asked.

Kal's face said it all. 'He's linked in with this, I know it.'

Ah-hah, yes, thought Marty, that was what had pushed Kal over the edge. And she knew how far Kal would go to save someone she cared for. No one would be able to stop her, not even Marty.

She kept her concentration on the uneven ground and made no comment about how Kal was pushing up the pace.

'I can see Dougie means a lot to you.'

'If they harm even one hair on his head, I swear I'll-'

To Marty it was obvious raw feelings were being stirred up in Kal about her father's crimes. She was the only one to know about all that. She must choose her words wisely.

Sweat started to run down Marty's back. 'We're going to make it. *You're* going to make it. You've got the brains to get them, I know you have.'

She stuck a hand in her pocket. 'Slow it down a little, will you? I thought you needed to take it easy on that leg of yours? Have a look at this.'

Avoiding a stretch of mud, Marty passed over her phone. On the screen was the line of symbols Kal had seen on the slab. Except they weren't carved in stone, they were carved on the wooden wall of a room.

'I found it online,' Marty said 'It's a perfect match with the ones you found in Ditchling. These were at a site where several young women were found dead in Arizona, USA.'

'Shit.'

196

'Exactly. It was an isolated place in the desert where two victims died from blood loss in the same way our women did.'

Marty was getting out of breath. 'They arrested the Arizona suspect six years ago and he committed suicide in police custody. End of story. Or so they thought.'

When she did her research, the link with America had given Marty the heebie-jeebies. As if a bunch of maniacs enacting sacrifices wasn't enough, it looked like they'd got copy-cats. Copy-cats who'd already evaded one police investigation.

Mud was flicking up from Kal's heels and Marty let her pull ahead.

Now Kal started pushing herself harder, pumping her arms to get up speed. The burn in her muscles helped to clear her head and she knew it was time to pull Marty out. The entire staff team at Clarence were suspects and Marty was in danger. Is that what happened to Jennifer? Her cover was blown and the killers moved in before she could get out? Or did she use her artistic abilities to draw the killers to her? Spinks had told her Jennifer was one of the best harp players in the country. She'd won national competitions as a child.

Kal shouted over her shoulder. 'It's time for you to get out.'

'No way. We haven't got what we came for. I'm your anchor woman.'

Kal was trying to out-run her and Marty picked it up to bring herself right up behind her friend.

'You need me there.'

'Except I don't need you dead.'

Kal tried to sprint away and Marty didn't let her. They pounded a flat stretch across the open common land, heading towards the road on the other side. By the time they reached it, both of them were hurting.

Kal was panting and she started walking in a circle. Damn it, she'd need to put an ice-pack on her knee. But it would have to wait, there was no time.

'The whole Clarence team could be working together, have you thought of that? They could all be part of some twisted, mind-fucked cult. This case is going to break soon, I can feel it and when it does, I need you by my side, not tied to some damn stone slab surrounded by freaking sickos.'

It was getting surreal. And yet it *was* real.

'Give me another twenty-four hours,' Marty said.

Kal didn't want to, and part of the reason was because if it came to a choice of saving Dougie or saving Marty, she knew what she would have to do.

She stabbed a finger at Marty's chest. 'No way.'

'I'm staying where I am.'

Kal knew she was angry and she didn't need anyone to tell her it was a bad sign. A sign she was ready to smash anyone and anything to get to Dougie before it was too late. Keep disciplined, she commanded herself, Marty's right, you've got to make it. Keep going and don't screw up, for Dougie's sake.

'This is getting crazy dangerous and you're too far away for me to keep my eye on you.'

'You don't need to. I can handle myself.'

Kal watched Marty stretching her hamstrings. She could see how badly Marty wanted it. Hell, Marty was doing great. Yet when the shit hits the fan, all hell could break loose and Marty would be the first in the firing line.

'I don't like it.'

'Another twenty-four hours and I promise I'll pull out.'

'You can be a real pain in the arse, did you know that?' Kal stopped pacing and wiped the sweat from her face. 'Twelve hours max. And that's all you're getting so don't argue.'

Marty had the good sense not to.

Kal gave her friend a glance. Marty was learning fast and she only hoped they'd be good enough.

Chapter Thirty-four

Ruth lay with her eyes closed. It was getting harder to remember the good things. It had all been snuffed out. As if a giant and ugly, mudslide had crept down to eat up a small village at its base. All the lights were gone, the laughter extinguished and Ruth was long since buried, long since suffocated. These days, all that was left were a few musical phrases and snatches of her favourite songs. When she couldn't hum to herself, she could hear them playing in her head. In lucid moments, Ruth realised that once her music went, she would be completely mad.

The ceremonial chamber was a scene from hell. Red symbols on the wall. The room dark as night. Light from the torches flickering to make the shadows loom like demons. And the catwalk, cold and smooth underfoot. Stretching ahead to an inclined table with attachments for pinning down the victim and tubing and metal to be inserted into sliced open arms. Fifty paces along the catwalk to the conclusion of a cold death.

A special knife for cutting. With a handle inlaid with mother of pearl. It might have been an object of beauty, or a collector's item, if it had not been a thing of cruelty.

And the smell. That was the worst. The smell of bloodlust and sweat and excitement. Mixing with the smell of death and the blood of her friends, and their terror. A cloying stink that couldn't be kept away, it stole into your soul and made you the dirtiest of dirty. Filthy forever.

In her mind, Ruth tried to run away from that stink. Because soon she knew she would be part of the red stream and part of the filth.

***

The three of them hadn't spoken for ages. Delilah was spending bouts of time memorising the paper. She wanted to get it perfectly right so not one single detail would be lost. Since she was eating so little, she lay down on her bed a lot with her eyes closed, trying not waste her energy.

The pyjamas she wore had become grubby. The ends of the sleeves were fraying, and the same for both ankles. Delilah no longer looked at herself in the mirror, for fear of what she might see; she didn't want to know how neglected and filthy and ravaged she'd become. As for her fingernails, she'd chewed them past the quick. She seemed to remember rats kept in captivity sometimes gnawed off their own legs and she could understand the mental torment which drove them to it. Because now she knew what mental anguish could do to you. It could twist your mind until you went back in on yourself.

Her mind kept drifting. Delilah often caught her thoughts wandering off and it scared her because she seemed to be doing it more and more. My god, how long had she been here? Her name hadn't come back to her yet, nor any details about her life before she came to this place. That frightened Delilah too. What if she never remembered?

On the bright side, none of the women had been taken out of their cells.

'Delilah?'

Ruth's voice was frail and yet musical. As if her music had become all she was.

Ruth had come to the bars of her cell and Kirsten too was taking notice.

'Uh-huh?' Delilah said.

'Could you pass me the paper and pencil, please?' Ruth said.

'Ruthie.' Kirsten's words were a mere whisper.

Delilah felt herself start shaking inside and she dare not meet Kirsten's eyes. They'd both thought Ruth was too far gone to realise a ceremony might be coming up. They'd both hoped Ruth wouldn't know.

Delilah took her time crawling on all fours to the bars and then stretching her arm as far as she could towards Ruth's cell.

A while later, Ruth handed it back.

Delilah crawled to her bed. Safe from prying eyes, she stared at the words for a long time and it felt as if her heart might break. Ruth had put her name at the bottom of the list, along with a little message and a line of kisses.

Chapter Thirty-five

When all three of them were summoned together, Kirsten gave Delilah a little nod. This was it.

Delilah moved as if she was in a dream.

Sitting on the bench, she watched as Kirsten took her shower in the glass cubicle. After, it was Ruth's turn. Then it was hers. Two silent, robed figures observed them.

Delilah tried to ignore how the masks stared as she shrugged off her pyjamas. There was nowhere to hide except in her own thoughts. Even under the running water, she could feel eyes on her, drinking her in, making her feel dirty. Her hands moved over the bones of her ribcage and those of her hips. How had she wasted so quickly?

As the hot water streamed down her back, Delilah closed her eyes. In her mind's eye, she went over the way they would soon take from the ante-chamber to the main room. Kirsten had described it very well. Delilah ticked off the details as she walked it in her imagination and her heart pounded. The moment was coming closer and closer.

This would be Delilah's first ceremony and Kirsten had told her all the details so she'd be able to keep her head together. She *must not* screw up.

After the showering they moved to a dressing area. The make-up bar was lavishly stocked and three evening dresses were laid out. The dress for Delilah was made of pale blue silk. As she picked it up her fingertips felt numb. Maybe it was an effect of the drugs? Or else a sickness? Or maybe she'd been here much longer than she realised? She had no idea and they had no way to mark the passage of time. The dress fell full-length to the floor.

Then the three of them sat side by side in front of a mirror lit by rows of lightbulbs like in a theatre dressing room. Ruth's hands trembled so much and Delilah's fingers were numb, so it was Kirsten who helped them both with their make-up. And all the while, Delilah went through the plan in her head, determined to not forget any detail of what she must do.

A huge hour-glass indicated how much time remained for them to prepare themselves. Delilah watched the sand spilling smoothly from the top to the bottom. It was strangely hypnotic, almost soothing.

Kirsten took her time, carefully applying eye shadow to her friends, mascara and blush, lipstick.

Delilah saw how even Ruth's eyelashes seemed to tremble. Ruth had become even more delicate. Was it because she anticipated the end? Delilah had to look away.

The masked figures were watchful and menacing. They made her want to scream.

When the last grains of sand ran into the bottom, they were signalled to stand.

It was then Delilah heard the beginning of a low, monotonous drone. The chanting had begun.

'You must steel yourself,' Kirsten had told her. 'If you go to pieces everything will be lost.'

Kirsten led the way in her crimson dress. She walked slowly and steadily out of the antechamber and they followed her in single file, bare feet silent on the floor. As they entered the next chamber, the chanting rose in volume and washed over them like a wave. Delilah started to shake. There were four of them altogether, not five like Kirsten said. Still, that pulled her down. That the enemy wasn't just one but many clumped together. All colluding and lying and sick in the head. In front of her, Ruth faltered and one of the figures raised its arm. There was a crack and a dark, snaking coil caught Ruth on the ankle. Ruth let out a gasp of pain. Delilah leant to steady her friend and Ruth shrugged her off, knowing Delilah risked a whiplash herself.

In the gloom, the catwalk stretched ahead of them lit on both sides by flickering torches.

Kirsten led them steadily down the catwalk, her head high and Ruth walked behind in her emerald green dress, so frail and light Delilah felt she might drift away. Concentrate, Delilah told herself. Do what you have to do. And get goddam out of this place.

At the far end of the room, she could make out the stone slab ready for the next victim.

Chapter Thirty-six

Stuart was an ordinary guy with an ordinary job. Yet he had an extraordinary secret.

Stuart had taken the afternoon off work so he could participate in the live link-up. It meant he'd needed to get up very early to fulfil his delivery schedule for the day and get home on time.

Most days Stuart hated his job. Today would ordinarily have been dull and boring had instead it had gone with a buzz. It made him glad he'd found a new interest. One that held the thrill of power over life and death.

Now Stuart sat, robed and masked, while the rest of the city went about its business. He'd said a cheery goodbye to the guy at the warehouse like he did any other day. That was a big part of the thrill too – to know no one suspected. That no one would ever discover him.

Stuart's whole attention was directed at the screen in front of him. This was a stroke of genius. In fact, he couldn't wait to start replicating it here in Detroit. Soon he would have the go-ahead and the guidance.

On the other side of the Atlantic, three beautiful women walked slowly along the catwalk. Stuart sweated as he willed himself to drink in every drop of this wonderful experience.

The first woman wore a crimson dress, with her hair piled on top of her head and wisps of it falling to frame her face. Behind her came a red-haired seductress. Stuart had already watched them both on video. Lastly, came London's new woman – a long legged blonde, who was certainly attractive. He looked forward to seeing her on video too one day.

In a few moments, he would make his choice and select a victim for tonight's Sacrifice. The honour would fall to him. Stuart almost wept with delight.

In a few more steps the women would be at the end of the catwalk and that would be his moment. And it was then that all hell broke loose and the screen in front of him went dead.

Chapter Thirty-seven

Kirsten had been on the catwalk before and she knew the ceremony by heart.

At her first one, Kirsten had still been in shock from being captured and incarcerated. She'd watched in horror when a woman she barely knew had been restrained on the table at the end. As they were locked back in their cells, they'd heard her screams.

At the times after that, she'd witnessed other women being frog-marched to the table. By then, it was women she knew and had grown to rely on. One of them had called out to Kirsten telling her to be strong. Another had an Irish accent and a wicked sense of humour which she'd tried to keep until the very end. Then at the last ceremony it had been Melissa who'd been taken and Ruth had to return later to mop up the pool of blood.

With each step, Kirsten neared the end of the catwalk. She could see the table and the straps. Staring straight ahead, she walked past the chanting figures. Who was behind those masks? What sort of monsters? She'd been tempted many times to snatch one of the masks away, to reveal the real, human face underneath. It had been Melissa who'd softly talked her out of it, saying there would only be one possible and terrible outcome. The masks would always win. It was obvious wasn't it?

Delilah was putting them all at risk with her idea of escape. Thing was, Kirsten didn't care anymore. She didn't care how futile the plan was. Ruth was the weakest and her friend was sure to be chosen tonight. And if she wasn't, and it was Kirsten's turn, then what did she have to lose by doing all she could to help Delilah?

The lights flickered on either side of the walkway, the bright torches throwing dancing shadows on the walls. The figures incanted the same insane words again and again. They were mad. Totally out of their minds. Kirsten did her best to block it out. The choice would be made once they got to the end. That would be the moment of greatest tension. The moment when she'd told Delilah to make her move. Would Delilah dare? Oh yes, thought Kirsten, she most definitely will and I shall do all I can to back her up. And she steeled herself in preparation.

Chapter Thirty-eight

Delilah was counting the steps.

Kirsten would soon reach the end. You've got to do it, she screamed at herself. *Just do it! Do it before it's too late.* It felt like taking a dive off a high cliff and feeling certain you'd be smashed to death on the rocks. *Go on! Jump!*

With as much will power as she could dredge up, Delilah screamed and lunged for one of the flaming torches.

It was a gamble and it didn't pay off. Kirsten had said it was one of many weak points in their plan and it didn't work because the torch was firmly attached.

In the seconds she had, Delilah couldn't wrench it free. She pulled and pulled as hard as she could and it wouldn't budge. Don't give up! She told herself. Keep trying.

Ruth stood immobile, paralysed and Kirsten also seemed rooted to the spot. Neither of them moved an inch to help her. One of the masked figures raised its arm and Delilah heard the crack of the whip. It caught her across the top of her chest, slicing like a razor. In pain and panic, she tumbled from the catwalk. The same figure now advanced towards her, raising its arm for a second strike and Delilah cowered.

Then, from nowhere, she heard her own voice in her head commanding her. *Throw it!* In one motion, she reached to the inside of her thigh where she'd strapped on a giant container of nail polish remover. In one motion, she threw it at the torches.

The flame ignited the spillage and Kirsten, who'd snapped out of her daze, did the same, throwing her container to the ground.

All hell broke loose. Kirsten launched from the stage onto the back of one of the figures and was trying to rip off its mask. The two of them struggled, and the robes of the figure caught fire.

Delilah smelt burning hair and there came a horrible scream. More flames leapt up where Kirsten crashed into a bundle of wires and plastic cabling. The place was going up in flames.

'Run!' Kirsten screamed at her.

Delilah had never been in that room before, yet she knew it as well as Kirsten knew it. She'd already memorised the location of her best bet at an escape route. Smoke began billowing from under the catwalk – dense and grey, it made it hard to breathe and difficult to see. Delilah started choking. A figure grabbed her and she kicked out. The person was strong and Delilah was weak but she was also desperate. Flames were racing along the floor and the noise was becoming deafening. Something fell from the ceiling and burst into flames as it landed, scattering their captors.

Delilah tried to crawl to the corner of the room where she knew she'd find the ventilation shaft. It was what Kirsten believed was their best route out and another weak point in their plan because they had absolutely no idea where it led to. There was no air anymore and Delilah fought for breath. In front of her eyes, she caught a bright, green flash as Ruth jumped from the catwalk and bolted for the corner. The smoke blotted Ruth from sight. Another of the masks was going after Ruth, and Delilah reached out, grabbed the ankle and brought the person crashing down. She was really choking now. It felt as if her lungs were on fire. She tried to crawl to the corner only the way was already blocked by flames. There was no air left. There was only heat and smoke. She was going to die. Delilah blacked out.

Chapter Thirty-nine

Ruth knew this ceremony would be the end for her. Actually, she wanted it. She'd even wondered if bleeding slowly to death might not be such a bad way out, as long as you could block out everything surrounding you.

Ruth had remembered her old life a while ago. First to come back had been her favourite songs – ones from her childhood and then ones she liked to sing on the streets. Then she remembered her mother who'd died of cancer and her father who'd died shortly afterwards of heart-ache. Ruth hoped the last thing she'd remember would be her absolute favourite song, which was by Nina Simone. In fact, it was a line from it that she'd written on the final paper. She would be happy for that to be her epitaph.

When Delilah shouted and grabbed for the torch, Ruth watched as if from afar, as if she was trapped in a dream, or rather, a nightmare. Then Kirsten jumped from the stage and Ruth stood still as a stone until the smoke became too thick and she started to cough. No one paid her any attention. After all, she was no threat to anyone. And that was her saving grace.

The heat built as fast as the fumes. Delilah had been clever to think of them taking the bottles of nail polish remover and tying them to the inside of their thighs. Ruth had heard Delilah telling Kirsten it was a fire accelerant, though Delilah said she had no idea how she knew that.

When Delilah threw hers, Ruth saw how the flames jumped up and Kirsten's had ignited the computing equipment. Now Ruth unstrapped her bottles and, as she ran, she lobbed them behind her.

Delilah was down. She'd never make it to the shaft. Ruth dived for the corner and yanked at the grille. They'd talked about it being another unknown because it was so unlikely it would be held in place with only two tiny screws like the one in Kirsten's cell. Except it was.

Ruth ripped it aside and dived headlong into the shaft. She'd take her chance down the shaft because she knew it was the last one she'd ever get.

Chapter Forty

Car headlights blinded her. Ruth tried to swerve to avoid them. Her eyes stung from the fumes and the smoke. She could hardly see. Her lungs burned and would not suck in the cold air. Car horns blared angrily and Ruth scooted down a side road. *Run, run, and don't stop. They're coming after you.*

What Ruth didn't know was their four tormentors were too busy using extinguishers to fight the fire, to chase after her. At that point, they didn't even realise she'd escaped and they were desperate to avoid the emergency services being called out for the fire. Meanwhile, Delilah and Kirsten were both unconscious on the floor.

Ruth had reached a high street. She swerved away from the hands of a man who tried to stop her. She didn't hear him calling after her that he could help.

There were more headlights and more blaring horns, and this time, Ruth was so disoriented she didn't know which way to go. People were running after her. She could see masks everywhere. They were going to take her back! *No! No!*

She swerved again. There came the screech of brakes and a *thud* of a body on metal, and Ruth bounced once on the windscreen and landed on the road.

Chapter Forty-one

Dr Samantha Singh said Ruth had been lucky. As a result of a car collision, Ruth could have suffered much more severe injuries. As it was, she had a fractured skull and several fractured ribs. They'd treated her for smoke inhalation and she also had burns to the backs of her legs which were sustained, said the doctor, prior to her impact with the vehicle.

More perplexing for the medical staff, was Ruth's incoherence and inability to tell them where she had been, what had happened to her and how she came to be running into the middle of a road in the first place.

She had a level of confusion Dr Singh did not attribute to her injuries. Before she'd allow Spinks to question Ruth, the doctor cautioned him about the patient's mental state. A psychiatric evaluation had been ordered. She also told Spinks Ruth had been malnourished long-term and that she'd told a nurse she'd been incarcerated against her will, though she later denied she'd said it.

Ruth showed no interest in Spinks. Her gaze was unfocused and aimed in the general direction of the wall. When he asked gentle questions, she would only tell him snippets about what had happened to her. Then she contradicted herself. She wept frequently, which meant Spinks could only progress at a snail's pace. After a few minutes, Dr Singh said she must call in specialist trauma support and Spinks nodded his agreement.

He was a very patient man, yet Spinks felt he was banging his head against a brick wall. Here they had a young woman who'd been reported missing two years ago, she'd been incarcerated and managed to escape, and the details she was able to tell him were sketchy and inconsistent.

Still dressed in her running gear, Kal almost banged into Spinks in the corridor.

'She's not up to questioning,' Spinks said. 'The counsellor has urged me not to press Ruth any further. It's a catch-22. By the time Ruth becomes stronger those other girls are going to be dead, that is, if they aren't already.' Spinks ran his hand through his hair.

Ruth had said she shared her captivity with two others, both of whom were blondes. It was the one decent piece of information she'd given and he'd tried to hold onto it, until she'd told him the others were called Delilah and Kirsten.

'I've only one question to ask her,' Kal said. 'May I?'

'You may as well,' Spinks said. 'And make it a good one.'

The young woman lay on her side, her cheek pressed into the pillow, red hair tied back in a pony tail. The usual sounds of the hospital filtered through from outside – muffled voices in the corridor, the clang of a trolley as it went past. Kal bent down and laid her hand lightly over Ruth's. She wasn't sure if Ruth even knew she was there.

'My name's Kal,' she said. 'I wanted to let you know I met a friend of yours… his name's Dougie.'

Ruth's eyelids fluttered at the sound of Dougie's name.

'He's been thinking about you.'

Spinks gave Kal a nod of encouragement.

Back at Dougie's group home, Simon and Dougie had shown Kal a recording of Ruth singing a Nina Simone song. They'd told her it was one of Ruth's favourites.

Kal selected it on her phone and held it close for Ruth to hear.

Ruth listened, then she smiled. 'Oh yes, I've been thinking about Dougie too.'

Kal turned to the nurse. 'Ruth is a talented singer and she plays the guitar and I get the feeling music could help a lot in her recovery.'

The nurse gave a nod of thanks.

Kal decided a few white lies were in order. She certainly wouldn't risk telling Ruth that Dougie had gone missing too.

'Dougie told me he wished you good luck. Does that mean anything to you, Ruth? Did it have anything to do with the people who took you?'

The song continued to play in the background and Ruth closed her eyes. Kal could see her short, jagged breathing.

It took a while for Ruth to open her eyes and when she did, both of them leaned forward to catch what she said.

'There was a window full of diamonds and Dougie's favourite was a dragonfly.'

Kal looked at Spinks and saw his flash of surprise. It mirrored her own.

'That's really helpful,' Kal said. 'Thank you, Ruth. Do you remember anything else?'

Ruth shook her head and started to cry. 'It's a blur. But I remember the sparkly dragonfly.'

***

The hospital staff had found a piece of paper stuffed into Ruth's underwear. Spinks showed Kal a photograph of it.

'It's a list of names and messages,' he said grimly.

Women had written their names on the paper. Kal's adrenalin level shot up and stayed there. She counted carefully – eleven names in all. It was five more than the body count Spinks had so far.

'Patrol are doing a door to door where Ruth was picked up. We might be lucky and find more witnesses. We've already got the driver and two passers-by, someone must know which direction Ruth was running from.'

Kal nodded. 'What about her lungs and the burns? Have there been any reports of a fire?'

'None so far and nobody else has come in with fire-related injuries. We're checking on the other London hospitals right now, so I should know soon if we've got any leads.'

In her mind's eye she imagined the eleven women who'd been held prisoner. She didn't doubt for a moment they were all now dead. This operation had been going on beneath the radar for years.

'You did well with Ruth,' Spinks said. 'What did you make of her last remarks?'

'Diamonds and a dragonfly? It could be a fantasy she's lost herself in to deal with her captivity. Or it could be key information. Your guess is as good as mine.'

'I'll ask the patrols to check for local jewellers.'

'Definitely, and let me know what they come up with.'

Spinks was about to send orders to his team when a message came in. He took one glance at the screen and took off for the end of the corridor. He called back to Kal.

'Come one. We just got a break. We've an address for Adam Mitchell's mother.'

Chapter Forty-two

Mrs Mitchell lived in a terraced house in Streatham. She never spoke to her neighbours. If anyone was ever curious enough to glance her way, she hoped they imagined her as an independent old woman who minded her own business.

Streatham suited her. It was packed with commuters who made the daily trip into central London and returned in the evenings, too tired to care about anything outside their own front door. This road offered Mrs Mitchell privacy and anonymity. It had been a perfect choice after Ditchling.

When the doorbell rang, she shuddered and pulled tight her little-old-lady shawl. She never had unexpected visitors.

Mrs Mitchell took her time shuffling down the hallway. She'd been watching the news and she knew the old barn had been found by the police, hell, half the country knew it. They'd already dug up the remains of several bodies and a line of press had to be kept back by a police cordon, with some members of the media resorting to camping in their cars. The national press were buzzing with it. She'd been waiting for the police to come knocking.

Leaning on the radiator, Mrs Mitchell caught her breath. The damned pneumonia last winter had left a scar on her health. She resented it, hated too the doctors and their platitudes. She was old and she was sick and she would never fully recover, only it didn't mean it was all over yet.

Apparently, the police were telling the press it was a major breakthrough in a current investigation. Well, good for them. It had taken the authorities decades to make the discovery. Which meant they were really not that smart.

A net curtain hung across the little window in the front door. Mrs Mitchell twitched it to the side. A man and a woman stood on her doorstep and the man was holding up an identity card. He was tall and wiry, and grey. The type to be sharp and to keep it hidden, she thought. She didn't like him.

Beside the man was a young, Indian-looking woman. Mrs Mitchell didn't like foreigners. Probably the girl was some sort of hopeless trainee. She slipped on the chain and opened the door a crack. Of course, she intended to let them in, but she wanted to play the helpless act to the full and she was certain it would work. It always did.

Kal took in the front room, letting her gaze sweep systematically across the furniture, the pictures, and the dust. There were no family shots. Rather, Mrs Mitchell had framed photographs of dramatic landscapes of somewhere that looked like the Scottish Highlands.

Mrs Mitchell sat on a large, comfortable chair and Kal noticed it didn't look like a worn out, favourite chair. Actually, it looked as if it were rarely used. That and the dust, made her think this room was for show and Mrs Mitchell spent most of her time somewhere else in the house. Kal took a deep breath, wondering if she'd catch a faint whiff of the same rank smell as at the Ditchling house. She didn't. Instead, the back of her throat got a blast of some kind of sticky, flowery air freshener.

'How can I help you officer?'

The woman gazed at Spinks with a mixture of awe and trepidation. There was a slight quiver in her chin.

Mrs Mitchell paused often, as if her memory wasn't as good as it used to be. She told Spinks she had no knowledge of the bodies and no idea of any activity at the barn. The barn was her husband's and she'd rarely ventured out there. When she was asked what her husband did in the barn, she said she always presumed it to be his smoking den. Then, when her husband left her for another woman, she'd not set foot in his stinking barn.

As for the house itself, Mrs Mitchell said she'd not been there in years, having left the property to her oldest son, Adam. She'd had no contact with Adam for over fifteen years.

Kal watched Mrs Mitchell closely. She noted the inflections of Mrs Mitchell's voice and her body posture and could only come to one conclusion – Mrs Mitchell was an accomplished liar. But it was so smooth and natural, so seamless, it suggested Mrs Mitchell was the type who actually lied to herself. The sort of person who reinvents reality the way they'd like it to be. That kind of lying went hand in hand with tucking away, or splitting off, a part of your persona you didn't want others to see. To Kal's mind it was a deep-seated condition and nothing to do with old age. It was more like a mental illness.

Kal felt certain the woman wouldn't fool Spinks either. Thing was, was Mrs Mitchell an accomplice to the crimes? They had no evidence to pin on her. Had she known? Had she been a witness? Or a victim of the real perpetrator?

That human remains were being unearthed in her back garden, brought on a prolonged bout of coughing and Mrs Mitchell buried her face in a lace handkerchief. Once she recovered, Mrs Mitchell told them her health had deteriorated due to pneumonia. She'd been hospitalised for several weeks during the winter and ill health now kept her housebound. Kal wondered if Mrs Mitchell knew how difficult that would make it to bring her in for questioning.

Spinks was digging in his pocket and he pulled out a photograph of Jennifer Morris.

'Do you recognise this woman?' he asked.

Mrs Mitchell held the picture up close and Kal saw how filthy the woman's fingernails were. She ran a dirty nail down Jennifer's face.

'She's a beauty, isn't she?' Mrs Mitchell said, looking Spinks straight in the eye.

Spinks didn't flinch, though Kal almost did, on his behalf. Was the woman baiting him? Was she very cleverly tugging his chain? Many serial killers got a kick out of playing with their interrogators. Giving hints and slipping in innuendos. Contradicting themselves and never, ever giving anything away that would be incriminating.

'Answer the question please, Mrs Mitchell,' Spinks said.

Mrs Mitchell again raked her nail across Jennifer's face and Kal leant forward and snatched back the photograph. It was then that something caught her eye. The edge of a white bandage was poking out from Mrs Mitchell's sleeve.

'No, I don't know her,' Mrs Mitchell said. 'Is she important to you?'

Kal caught a whiff of danger. She'd been so intent on examining Mrs Mitchell, she hadn't realised Spinks might be giving off weird signals. The same strange signals she'd picked up when he first told her about the case, the ones that showed how important Jennifer was to him. Shit. She moved quickly to deflect Mrs Mitchell's attention.

'Have you been injured? I notice you've a bandage on your arm.'

'It was a silly little mishap while I was getting out of bed the other morning. Unfortunately, when you get to my age, falls happen all too easily.'

Mrs Mitchell gave a cold smile and Kal returned it.

A fall Mrs Mitchell, or a burn? She thought to herself.

She was dying to inspect the rest of the property. It would be easy to engineer an excuse, like needing to use the bathroom. The only thing was, it would mean leaving Spinks on his own and that worried her, which was stupid. Spinks was experienced and seasoned and he didn't need her to shield him from an old woman. Nevertheless, Kal felt protective. Mrs Mitchell wasn't what she seemed and the woman was far too perceptive. It spelled danger. So Kal sat back and let Spinks continue his questioning.

The room reminded Spinks of the old house in Ditchling with its rotting carpets. He wasn't sure how that could be, since apart from a thick layer of dust, the furniture and fittings appeared to be in a good state. There was no filth in sight. It was almost as if Mrs Mitchell herself gave off the smell, he thought. Then he chastised himself for letting his imagination get the better of him.

Spinks was a fact-based detective. He filed all the details of a case away, until they made sense and told him their own story. In his long years of experience, this method always worked. It was a matter of having the patience and the endurance to see it through – and Spinks had plentiful supplies of both.

When Mrs Mitchell ran her finger down Jennifer's photograph, Spinks tried not to focus on it. He didn't shift in his seat a millimetre, because he'd spent years training himself in the interrogation room and could control his own impulses and his own expression. He could make himself a blank sheet. In those few seconds, he realised he should have told Kal the truth about Jennifer from the beginning. Only it was too late for that now.

The team had recovered the remains of four women and one man at the Ditchling site. Their identities would take longer to establish and Mrs Mitchell was expertly shifting the accusations towards her husband. If Spinks was a betting man, which he wasn't, he'd wager the male skeleton would turn out to be this woman's husband – the husband Mrs Mitchell just told him had absconded when Adam was a toddler.

She wasn't giving anything away. Streatham was located several miles from where Ruth had been picked up, so there was no way Ruth had been imprisoned in this house. They had nothing on the woman. Not yet. Time to move on.

Mrs Mitchell watched them walk along her garden path and watched Detective Chief Inspector Spinks open the little gate onto the street. She let the net curtain fall back into place.

She'd handled the intrusion well. All the police had was a cold, cold trail that would lead them nowhere. That taciturn Indian girl wasn't much of a threat. The detective was another story. No, Mrs Mitchell didn't like that detective. He oozed too much cool confidence. He had far too much self-assurance and poise, as if he always felt sure he would get his man.

She had to sit for a few moments for her rage to settle. These days, the fury and bile that made her who she was, also made her hands shake.

Mrs Mitchell dialled a number and it rang three times.

The person who picked up on the other end waited for her to speak first.

'It was clean. They don't have the slightest clue what's going on.' She gave a mirthless laugh. 'However, I think it's time to take out a little insurance.'

There was another silence on the other end, as her subject waited for his orders. She didn't expect comments from her sons, only servitude. She leant back in her chair, comfortable with her own power.

'It seems our new guest is someone Detective Spinks values very highly indeed. In fact, I'd be willing to bet she's a police officer.'

Mrs Mitchell tapped the side of the phone.

'It seems we made a serious error of judgement taking her as a guest,' she said.

Mrs Mitchell's face was contorting with rage and it made her look like a gargoyle. On the other end of the line, Adam held completely still. He didn't need to remind himself of her merciless nature. She still held absolute power, for now at least. He made sure he kept his lips firmly shut.

'I think we need to take Inspector Spinks out of the picture,' the Grand Master said, her voice icy. 'This is what I want you to do.'

Chapter Forty-three

Delilah coughed so deeply and so hard, she brought up blood. They slung her back in her cell and left her there on the floor, where she passed out.

When she awoke, her lungs were on fire. Every tiny breath felt like agony. She remembered the searing heat of the flames, and the thick, acrid smoke. Using an accelerant had been a stroke of genius. Without it, the fire would never have taken hold so quickly.

Trying to breathe shallowly, she rolled inch by agonising inch onto her side. Had Ruth really escaped? Ruth had got to the corner, yes, she'd seen that happen. Or was it in her dreams? No, she'd seen it, hadn't she? Right now, Ruth would be telling her story to the police and help would be on its way.

She had to have water. Delilah crawled to the sink at the back of her cell. It took an age to get there and an age more to pour some out. Her throat was raw and she had to take little sips.

She lay there, slumped on the floor. Delilah hadn't succeeded in getting out, but if Ruth had made it, it would have been worth it. One thing she did not want to do was check to see if Ruth was in her cell. Because she was afraid that she might be. Then all Delilah's hopes would be dashed.

It took her a long time to bring up the courage to make the journey to the bars. She dragged herself by her elbows. When it got too much, she stopped and lay face down on the floor and waited until she could continue. When she finally arrived, she gathered her strength and forced her face off the ground.

'She's not there.' It was Kirsten who spoke. 'She got out of the chamber, I saw her, and unless they've recaptured her, Ruthie got away.'

Hot tears spilled from Delilah's eyes.

'I've been waiting and waiting for you to come round,' Kirsten said. 'You got me so scared, I thought you might-'

Delilah made herself speak, pushing the words out in a hoarse whisper that felt like a knife.

'I'm alive and kicking. Out of all of us, it was Ruth who made it.'

'Yeah, I know, weird isn't it? I saw her leaping from that damn catwalk like she was a bird about to fly.'

Kirsten laughed and Delilah couldn't because it hurt too much. Then she noticed Kirsten cowering.

Kirsten turned away, though not fast enough because Delilah saw the huge black and bubbling swathe on Kirsten's body where there should have been skin. Oh god. A panic tried to rush in.

'You're burned.'

Kirsten didn't bother to deny it. 'I don't care. Little Ruthie got out and that's all that matters.'

Delilah nodded automatically. Oh god, her friend must be in agony. Burns like that needed covering. They needed emergency treatment. And what about infection? Fluid loss? Shock? Kirsten needed a hospital. Delilah tried to sound positive.

'All we've got to do is sit back and wait for help to arrive.'

'Uh-huh,' Kirsten said and she rested her head on her arm.

Now that Delilah was awake, Kirsten felt better.

When they'd first brought Kirsten back to the cells, it had been so agonising she didn't think she'd be able to stand it. The thought of Delilah never waking up had made it worse. At least now she was not alone.

Earlier she'd got the shakes from head to foot. And then she'd felt cold. What had that been about? And now she began to feel so horribly hot. Waves of sweat kept rolling down her.

In her mind's eye, Kirsten imagined Ruthie in her emerald-green dress flying off the catwalk. She saw Ruth flying through the air, across London, high above the rooftops, peaceful and happy and free. She smiled. She was starting to feel strange. Kirsten closed her eyes.

Chapter Forty-four

The chest freezer had space for two bodies. Adam stared at Tom lying in the ice with his arms crossed across his chest. He pushed the stiff cadaver as far to one side as possible and hefted in the inert body of Samson.

Samson had been burned when his robes caught fire. He required urgent hospitalisation and that would mean plenty of awkward questions and a trail that led back to The Lodge. Therefore, the Grand Master decided it was time for Samson's end.

'You won't be coming on our new adventure, Brother.' Adam said.

It had been his mother's idea to recruit Samson and Samson had been useful. He'd enjoyed taking part in their activities. Then his mother had used Samson. One of Samson's women had tricked Inspector Taylor into sex and the woman fed Taylor snippets of information about Samson's competitor's drug deliveries. It had given Taylor a feeling of success and kept him focused away from Samson's own networks and far, far away from The Lodge.

Adam slammed the freezer shut and locked it.

The Ceremony chamber was ruined and all their equipment useless. Yet tonight would not pass without a victim.

Of the two remaining guests, one was almost as badly burned as Samson. She wouldn't last long. She'd die a horrible, slow death in her cell. As for the second guest, the new Grand Master had special plans for her. A Sacrifice was being organised for midnight. By the old methods.

Everything would change tonight. The wheels were in motion and the new leader was ready to seize power. And it was the perfect time to move location. The two of them would wrap up here and set up in Detroit.

Chapter Forty-five

The team had received a torrent of calls from the public. Everyone searching for a lost relative, every psychic, and every nutter, they all wanted to talk to the police about the remains being unearthed in Ditchling. Sifting the information required significant resources. The chief had been forced to assign three detective constables to log the calls and pinpoint any decent leads.

It was good luck Adam Mitchell's call was picked up by Detective Constable Diane Colt. DC Colt had a nose for this type of thing. She could sift the good from the bad and from the time-waster. That's why DC Colt knew straight away this caller was an important one. She ran into Detective Chief Inspector Spinks' office, her knuckles barely grazing the door before she barged in.

Spinks was startled. He whipped off his reading glasses.

'There's a call come through from somebody claiming to be Adam Mitchell.' DC Colt was breathless. 'Sir, I think you should take it.'

***

In DCI Spinks' view, it was the foundation of good policing to treat all victims of crime with equal consideration. One victim should never be more important than another. One person should not call on his reserves, not to mention his time, more than another. Which was why his refusal to turn away Mrs Stanislova over the last year had puzzled his team so much. She still came for her meetings and Spinks pushed aside his other responsibilities and sat with her. On one occasion the two of them had been together for almost half an hour. His team knew because they'd timed it.

There were no rumours because Spinks' stellar reputation killed them. He was respected and all the younger detectives hoped one day they'd turn out to be like him. So there was no speculation amongst his staff, simply confusion.

It was only Spinks who knew how Mrs Stanislova's face haunted his nightmares.

Before he closed his eyes at night and when he woke up in the morning, it was Mrs Stanislova who was imprinted on his retina. And her pain, which was a mother's pain, ripped at him.

These days he couldn't stand the smell of coffee. It made him think of her settee covered in coffee spills. He was taking a detour through a neighbouring team's office to avoid the coffee machine.

Spinks was not able to confide in anyone. He'd made a solemn promise and he intended to keep it at whatever cost.

Pushing the glass of lemonade away, Spinks felt the beginnings of a headache. He watched the pub door, waiting for the arrival of Adam Mitchell.

He'd recognised Adam's voice on the phone. It was as if all the years fell away and Spinks was again facing his suspect across a plastic table in an interrogation room. Spinks recalled, or thought he did, the swagger in Mitchell as he pushed back his chair and walked to the door when they'd been forced to release him.

In the brief call, Adam Mitchell said he had information about Jennifer and he was willing to trade for her safe release.

He should not have come here alone and he should certainly have informed the team of his movements. This pub was off his patch. But he didn't care. With Jennifer's life at stake, Spinks was willing to risk his career, his reputation, and even his own life.

Chapter Forty-six

Simon stood outside Dougie's empty room.

They kept Dougie's door ajar so residents could peer in if they wanted to. Simon was pretty certain he was the person who peered in the most. Someone had placed a box of tissues on a little table outside the door and Simon grabbed a handful, wiped his eyes and blew his nose.

A London-wide alert had been issued and Simon feared the worst. Dougie wasn't capable of being alone for so long.

A colleague came bounding up the stairs with a visitor in tow.

'Someone to see you, Si.'

Kal stepped out from behind.

'Dougie?' Simon said. He couldn't stifle the hope in his voice.

'I'm sorry, I don't have any news. We're all working flat out, so let's keep positive, okay?' Kal put her arm around his shoulder. 'There's something important you can help me with. Do you have copies of the digital shots from Dougie's camera?'

Dougie's room reflected his personality and Kal caught the faint scent of lavender. There were posters of cats and plenty of Dougie's photographs of the residents and staff out on trips.

It turned out Dougie diligently kept copies of all his pictures on hard drive.

'The police have found Ruth,' she told Simon. 'She's in hospital in a bad way and she told me something really important. Her exact words were, "There was a window full of diamonds and Dougie's favourite was a dragonfly." Does it mean anything to you? Did Dougie ever talk about diamonds or a dragonfly?'

Ever since he ran into Kal down by the river, Simon had had his suspicions. Kal wasn't what she seemed and yet he trusted her. Now it seemed she was working with the police.

'Yes! Dougie had a special brooch.'

He picked up Dougie's pillow but there was nothing there.

'He always kept it under here and he didn't tell me anything about it. I discovered it one day by accident. I'm pretty certain it was a gift from Ruth.'

Kal nodded, her dark eyes unreadable.

'You're not homeless are you?' Simon said.

'Listen, I haven't got time for long explanations, and before you accuse me of anything I had no intention of misleading Dougie. I genuinely liked him and I'm not going to abandon him… even after this is all over. I'm working with DCI Spinks and that's all you need to know. I'm a friend, I promise.'

'I know you are.' Simon sat on the bed. 'Has the brooch got something to do with why Dougie went missing?'

'My guess is Dougie has key information about Ruth's disappearance. She was kept prisoner and we need to locate where. Other women are being held, most likely at the same place she escaped from. And Dougie might be there too, at least, that's what I'm betting. It's all right Simon, I'm on to it, please don't panic. I need you thinking clearly.'

Simon tried to take deep breaths.

'Dougie only wore the brooch once as far as I can remember. It was the first Christmas after Ruth disappeared. It was very pretty and sparkly and exactly the type of thing Dougie would like. We took plenty of pictures that day.'

He went to the computer and, after a few minutes, pulled up shots of the residents at Christmas dinner.

'This is it,' Simon said.

He zoomed in on Dougie's jumper and Kal inspected the dragonfly. It was a lovely piece of jewellery.

'Are you sure Dougie wasn't given this by somebody else? Maybe a family member?'

'I'm certain. Dougie's parents died ages ago. He has a sister who lives in Australia and she's generous with money only she never sends gifts. She'd rather transfer a couple of thousand for Christmas and birthdays and we dip into it whenever he needs something. That's how Dougie bought such an expensive camera. The dragonfly brooch must have come from Ruth. And it was special, that's why he kept it under his pillow.'

Kal gave Simon a piercing look and he tried not to cringe. God help any criminals that got in her way, he thought.

'Think about this next question very carefully,' Kal said.

Simon couldn't help nodding.

'Do you have idea where it was bought?'

He really wished he had. Simon searched his memory and all the times he'd walked with Ruth and Dougie. They hadn't gone anywhere except Ruth's usual busking points.

'Ruth always came here! I've absolutely no idea where they might have got it.'

'It's okay,' Kal said soothingly. 'If you don't know it's not your fault. From the way Ruth told me about it, I got the impression Dougie made a choice. That she took him somewhere and he picked it out himself.'

'Wait a minute. Dougie took pictures of most places he went to and he took hundreds of Ruth. Maybe the answer's right here.'

Simon waved at the computer screen.

Kal slapped him on the back. 'Can you get searching or do you want me to ask DCI Spinks to get someone on it?'

'I can do it faster. I'm the one who knows when Ruth was around.'

Kal was already heading out the door. 'Great. Get started straight away and send me through anything, and I mean anything, as soon as you find it.'

She turned and stared Simon straight in the face. 'It could be a life saver.'

Chapter Forty-seven

Marty determined to stick at it until she had answers. She downed a giant bowl of muesli. Then she pulled the blinds on her third-floor apartment and settled in front of her screen.

Spinks had sent over the police files from Arizona and Marty set herself the task of finding the needle in the haystack.

The American case had been cracked as a result of a tip-off from a tourist. The tourist had been driving across the Arizona desert in a four by four. He'd got lost and spent the night in his car. In the morning, as he prepared to set off, he'd spotted something discarded on the ground. It was a woman's dress. A few metres away, he found a single woman's shoe. The man was alarmed. Was someone lost? Was a woman wandering in the vast expanse of the desert? It was surely a chance in a million he'd pulled up at the right place.

As soon as he had a signal, he made an emergency call and the authorities sent a car. The patrolmen located a homestead with its own water well. The place expertly hidden and inside the house, the police made a gruesome discovery. They found three women incarcerated in cells and two of the victims were already dead.

There were plenty of photos of the women and Marty cringed as she inspected them.

Flipping to the coroner's report, she read of the verdict of death by ex-sanguination. The women's wrists had been cut along the longitudinal line. Marty's own wrists tingled as she read how they'd bled to death in the same way as the victims in London.

The third woman in the cells had been in a near-death state. It had taken Chloe Carter months to recover and she was left with damage to her nervous system and organs, and crippling pains which the doctors said she would have for life.

It was this woman's witness statement which led the police to charge Alfredo Manson. Manson was arrested. But the case never went to trial because Manson killed himself while in police custody.

Marty skimmed the visuals of the homestead set against the stark, Arizona landscape. It was a functional timber house which Manson said he constructed himself. Then she stared at Manson's face a good while. He had trimmed hair and dark eyes. Manson's face was normal looking. He was of average height, average build. She read he had average education and worked security in a mall. She wondered what made him into such an evil person.

The survivor, Chloe, was a ballet dancer. Chloe told how she'd been invited to an audition by Manson, only to find herself faced by a masked maniac who wanted to film her naked, in fact, naked and dancing classical ballet. She was drugged and ended up imprisoned. Chloe was held for fourteen months.

So, if Alfredo Manson was the perpetrator and he killed himself six years ago, what was the link? First in Ditchling fifty years ago, then in London and Arizona both going on at the same time, and now on-going in London? There had to be a connection.

Alfredo Manson admitted to abducting the women. He'd admitted to killing two of them and attempting to kill the third. What he hadn't been willing to tell was whether other bodies had been dumped or hidden elsewhere. He also denied the collaboration of others in the abductions or the murders.

Then there were the problems with Chloe's statement. If the case had ever gone to court it would have rested on Manson's confession because doctors found mind-altering drugs in Chloe's system which meant her testimony was deemed inadmissible.

Substances had been given to the women in their food. As Chloe regained her mental stability, she changed her statement several times. She contradicted herself on everything, including the number of perpetrators involved. It started out as a three, then it dwindled to two, and by the end, Chloe was adamant it was only one person.

Yes, thought Marty, but the same crimes in different places says otherwise. What if the link *is* a person? What if someone went from London to Arizona? That person wasn't Manson because he was now dead and the crimes were still continuing in London. Did it mean a second person, or persons, got away from the States?

Marty was running on adrenalin. She paced the lounge. Should she track down the interviewing officers? Speak to the coroner? No, she couldn't mess around. Marty checked the time. 9.30pm.

Spinks, Kal and Marty all agreed the perpetrators would assume Ruth could tell them more than she actually could. They'd likely sacrifice any women they had and clear out.

Marty pulled up a search for Chloe Carter. There were several American women with that name who had active social media accounts. Only one of them had attended the Academy of Ballet in Houston and gone on to train as a professional dancer.

Things had moved on for Chloe. She'd studied at law college and now worked as a legal assistant for a top firm of lawyers. She had a one-year old baby daughter. It would be day time for Chloe. If Marty was lucky, she might catch her at work.

Calling a complete stranger to talk about horrible events of six years ago was firmly out of Marty's range of experience. She went through it in her mind. Information Chloe could give was vital. So – how should she open the conversation? What could she say that could possibly stop Chloe slamming down the phone?

There was only one way – she must be honest. Being herself and presenting the situation clearly should be enough credentials.

After speaking to a main receptionist, Marty found herself waiting for Chloe Carter to answer her desk phone. Marty smeared her sweating palms down her jeans.

'This is Chloe Carter.'

'I'm really sorry to bother you. I'm calling from London, England and I really need your help. I just read your witness statements and I'm working on a current case which bears a terrible resemblance to the incarceration you suffered.'

Mrs Carter sucked in a breath. It took a few seconds for her to regain her poise.

'Are you a reporter? I've nothing to say. And if you're calling from the British police, which I don't think you are, you'll have to go through official channels.'

'A woman managed to escape.' Marty blurted it out. 'She's in a terrible state and she can't tell us much. There are two other women we still haven't found. Please, we need your help.'

'Who exactly are you?' Mrs Carter's voice was clipped, legal-assistant style.

'My business partner is working with the police. She's a skilled investigator and I'm, er, her back up. When I read through the police files it jumped out at me there's a link between the cases. I don't mean someone doing a copy-cat crime, I mean an *actual person* who was involved in Arizona must have a link with the killings here.'

Chloe said nothing and Marty took it as her cue to press on.

'You said you thought there was more than one person involved. I know you changed your mind later on and I wanted to ask you why.'

'It was so long ago, I really don't think-'

'Mrs Carter please, you're our only hope of finding the two missing women before it's too late.'

Chloe must have been standing up, because Marty heard her collapsing into a chair.

'You sound genuine so this had better not be some kind of sick hoax.'

'I assure you it isn't.'

'It's highly irregular to phone me out of the blue and since you placed this call you'll know I work for a top legal firm. If parts of this conversation are ever used in a public way, or indeed *any way* I don't like, you'll find yourself facing litigation. I have your number and I can find your details anytime I want. Am I making myself clear?'

'Crystal clear, Mrs Carter.' Marty's hopes were sinking fast. She obviously didn't have the magic touch. Marty heard another sigh on the other end of the line.

'I hardly think about it these days and I can thank my lovely daughter for that. She keeps me so busy. Except… in the odd dark moment it all floods back. No one can understand, not if they've never lived it.'

Chloe Carter went silent and Marty waited.

'You said a woman managed to escape. What's her name?'

Marty didn't want to blow it. Probably best to keep her replies minimal in case she said the wrong thing.

'Ruth.'

'That's a pretty name and biblical too. She must have been so brave. How did she get out?'

'There was an incident instigated by the women. They were taken out of their cells and made to parade

246

on a catwalk and they took their chance to create a fire as a diversion.'

There came a long silence and Marty wondered what nightmare images she'd triggered in Chloe Carter's mind.

'Are you certain there's really a link? Were there people in masks?'

'I'm as certain as I can be, given we're working in the dark and- wait a minute, you said people plural?'

'No I didn't, well, yes I think I did. It's all so muddled up. You see, they gave us stuff to keep us confused and docile. It messed with our thinking.'

'Yes, I read you were drugged and that's part of the pattern here too. And at the beginning, you were telling the police there was more than one person.'

'I'm so sorry, I really wish I could help only I'm afraid I don't have anything useful to add. I told it all so many times and I was in a mess. The person wore a mask and long black robes. When I think back I sometimes see more than one of them but I sort of convinced myself it was an illusion. You know, like when you're drunk and you're not sure how many fingers are being held up? Not that I'm ever drunk. I've not had a drop of alcohol and I never will. Not after that.'

'Mrs Carter,' Marty said, her voice heavy. 'What if it wasn't an illusion or a trick of your mind. What if there really was more than one person? I know the Arizona authorities didn't see it that way but my own thoughts point to that conclusion. Are you really certain Manson worked alone?'

'Everything happened so fast during the run-up to the trial. And the police were adamant they'd caught the perpetrator and it was a big win for them here in the press. A big political win too. Manson confessed and when he killed himself there was nothing for them to pursue. Maybe that influenced how I thought about it in some way…'

'And if they were wrong and someone escaped justice?'

'Oh gosh, please don't say that. It gives me the shivers. The women I was with, they were dear to me and then to wonder if someone might have got away with it… What happened to us… It doesn't bear thinking about.'

Marty paused. She could sense Chloe Carter delving back into her bad memories.

'And then if that person continued in another place… it would be unbearable to imagine.'

'I don't think I'm imagining it, Mrs Carter. I think the Arizona crimes were seeded from the UK and if that's the case, the person who took the idea to America most likely came back here.'

Again there was silence down the phone and Marty wondered if Chloe had lost the plot.

'I saw a trauma counsellor,' Chloe finally said. 'In fact, I still see her occasionally. One of the reasons for that, and this isn't in any of the records and I'd appreciate if you kept it confidential…'

'Of course.'

'…one of the reasons I still see my therapist is because my mother left us when I was little and I was brought up by my father. My mother was an alcoholic and something came out in the counselling sessions which I couldn't make any sense of. You see, in my nightmares, my mother's face keeps getting mixed up with the face of the captor. It was my biggest hurdle to recovery because I kept imagining my own mother was the masked figure who visited us daily in the cells. Worse than that, it was her who was in charge directing everything and she was called "Master". I know that sounds crazy. My therapist has explained it all to me and it's not as bad as it sounds. Apparently, there's a sound psychological explanation for my subconscious confusing the two of them. Something to do with them both being abusive experiences. Anyway, that's not why I'm telling you. I'm telling you because suppose, just suppose, it wasn't simply my mind mixing things around? I've no doubt of Manson's guilt because he was the one who took me to the audition, but what if you're right? What if someone else was involved?'

Marty clutched the phone.

'What if someone else was involved and my mind has been trying to tell me all along that person *was a woman*?'

Chapter Forty-eight

Delilah wanted to hold Kirsten in her arms. She wanted it so desperately, it was killing her. She wanted to stroke Kirsten's hair and tell her everything would be all right. Instead, she watched helpless and trapped behind the bars, whilst her friend suffered.

Kirsten was dying. She spoke in whispers about her mother and her sisters and other things Delilah couldn't understand.

Since the fire, there'd been no sign of the masks. There had been no sounds from above, no approaching footsteps, no food. If only one of them would come, Delilah would plead with them to take care of Kirsten. She'd promise them anything and mean it. Delilah found herself begging for them to appear.

She realised it had been too long. Ruth must not have got out. They must have killed her. Which meant there was no help coming.

The funny thing was, and it was funny, which made her feel she was finally going mad herself – she'd started to remember bits about her life. She knew her name was Jennifer Morris. She knew she was a police officer. And she knew they were going to die and that she would have to watch Kirsten die first.

'It's all right Kirsten, hold on. Help is on the way,' she lied.

'We didn't give in, did we?' Kirsten whispered. 'They didn't get the better of us.'

'No,' Jennifer said. She had no strength left for tears. 'No, my darling they didn't. They never got the better of us.'

Chapter Forty-nine

By the time Spinks arrived in Streatham, his shirt was glued to his back with sweat. Discarding his jacket, he ran the few steps to Mrs Mitchell's house.

Adam Mitchell was playing games. Spinks had sat in the pub for fifteen minutes before he'd received a text with instructions. Mitchell told Spinks to go to his mother's house. He'd told him to come alone and to not inform anyone, and that he must arrive by 9.45pm if he wanted Jennifer to stay alive.

They had a specialised unit to deal with demands like this and to handle hostage situations and negotiation. Spinks knew it would take too long to mobilise those resources. He also knew the risks involved in using them. No, with Jennifer's life at stake, he would handle this alone.

Due to heavy traffic, Spinks arrived at the rendezvous at 9.50pm. If he'd been a man prone to cardiac arrest he'd have probably had one on the way over.

The front door had been left ajar. There were splatters of blood on the floor and the trail led down the passageway. His mind was so programmed to conserve evidence, Spinks walked close to the wall, careful to avoid the drops as he followed them into the house.

Upstairs, Mrs Mitchell tried to pull herself up, slipping on the sides of the bath. The liquid lapped her chin and she sank back, unable to muster the strength to keep herself above the waterline. Her mind was wandering. Blood loss did that to you as the brain slowly starved of oxygen. It made bleeding to death blissful or so they said. The bath was warm and comfortable. Perhaps she shouldn't fight it, perhaps she should simply let herself drift off to sleep. Her own flesh and blood had turned on her. The fucking bastards. And they'd whispered one thing in her ear as they pushed her down.

The sound of someone coming up the stairs roused her and brought back a spark of life.

'Help me,' Mrs Mitchell called, her voice no louder than a whisper.

Spinks paused at the top of the stairs, trying to identify which room the noise came from. Unlike the downstairs lounge which he and Kal had seen, the upper floor of Mrs Mitchell's house was filthy. It had the same bad smell as the house in Ditchling.

In Ditchling, the crime scene team had now identified the filth as a mixture of the blood of several victims and other human fluids, mixed with everyday dirt. The team speculated how blood had regularly been transported inside the house. In fact, transported in a way that no one cared how much slopped onto the floor in the process. Also, the bath and its drainage outlets had tested positive for blood and DNA, as if the bath had been used as a means of disposal. Or of storage. The

Mitchell family house had really turned into a house of horrors.

Spinks wished he had a SWAT team at his back. He'd walked into situations like this before and it was always a reassurance to have a crack sniper a mere whisper away on a secure link.

He trod a few more steps and then stopped. He heard a noise and tried to decide if the sound might be Jennifer. He could not tell.

'Mitchell, where are you? We talk face to face or we don't talk at all.'

Spinks' voice was hard. He must make his own demands and not let the other side call all the shots.

Continuing along the landing, the soles of his shoes stuck slightly with each step. The sound had come from here. Would he find Jennifer dead or on the verge of death? Would Mitchell have a knife at her throat? Or might he be in the process of cutting Jennifer's wrists? Spinks steeled himself, sweat running into his eyes and the terrible stench cloying at the back of his throat.

As he entered the room, Spinks felt his mind reeling. Mrs Mitchell lay in a bath of red liquid.

He was flooded with a mixture of relief and horror and disgust.

Mrs Mitchell saw the emotions race across Spinks' face. It gave her a moment of pleasure. As he leant over her, she noticed his shrewd eyes and greying hair. And she saw how concern for her now dominated his thinking. By now, she'd lost so much blood she felt almost giddy. Did she have enough strength for one final act, just as they'd whispered to her? Could she go out in style?

Spinks reached to Mrs Mitchell's arm and lifted it out of the tub. The wrist had a longitudinal slash running from the hand to half-way up the forearm. The old woman was bleeding to death. He wrapped one hand around the slash and squeezed hard and reached to his pocket with his other hand. She still had a chance and once he'd made the call he could stem both arms. He also needed to drain the bath so she didn't damn well drown in the meantime.

Spinks had moved into the familiar groove of response-to-an-emergency. He'd expected to be confronted by Adam Mitchell using Jennifer as a physical bargaining chip. He'd expected to be negotiating for her life. He'd expected Mitchell to be desperate, on the edge, that maybe Mitchell anticipated incriminating evidence at Ditchling linking him to the crimes and he wanted to try to pin the blame on someone else. He'd been prepared to talk Adam down, using his experience to find a way in. At least now he could hope to find Jennifer alive.

Spinks took a quick, reflexive glance behind him before he made the call. The room was empty and no sounds came from the rest of the house. It wasn't until he had the phone at his ear that he felt the puncture under his ribs. He looked down in surprise. Mrs Mitchell's other arm wasn't slit. She'd pulled it out of the bath and stabbed a knife into his belly, all the way up to the hilt. He caught the look of triumph on her face, as he staggered back, the handle sticking out of his gut.

Spinks had only one thought – that relief for Jennifer had made him stupid.

Footsteps sounded on the stairs. Unhurried, confident footsteps.

Spinks knew better than to pull out the knife. It could make as much damage going out as it had going in. The pain made it impossible to stay on his feet. On his knees, he pressed one large hand around the blade and into his own flesh to try to stem the flow. Blood spilled between his fingers. His phone had fallen a short distance away and he dragged himself towards it. Adam Mitchell arrived just in time to kick it away from Spink's fingertips.

'Now, now, that's enough of that,' Adam Mitchell said.

Adam Mitchell used his foot to flip Spinks onto his back.

Mitchell jerked his head towards his mother. 'She's extraordinary isn't she? Barking mad of course, and ruthless. I learned everything I know from her. What's the matter? Cat got your tongue?'

Mitchell laughed and Spinks could hear an edge of insanity in it.

'We told her she could have one last victory. Taking life was always her thing.'

Mitchell sat on the side of the bath and stared at his mother. She'd slipped down so her mouth was below the surface and he pushed on her head to submerge her nose.

'It's time for her to go. Her life's work was establishing The Lodge but she was getting weak. We have to get rid of her.'

Adam Mitchell waited until no more bubbles broke the surface, then he walked back to Spinks.

'And you will never see your precious Jennifer again.'

Under Spinks, a dark pool was spreading on the filthy carpet.

'Where is she?' Spinks asked.

'Somewhere you'll never find her. You should have put me away when you had the chance, old man.'

Mitchell crossed back to the bath and lifted his mother's arm. He let it flop back and Spinks heard the splash.

'She used to bathe in their blood, did you know that? My brother Tom and I had to cart gallons of it up to the top of the house in Ditchling so she could immerse herself. She used to let us watch her, then she'd walk around naked, continually smearing herself with it. It was a fascinating upbringing for a young boy.'

Spinks felt a terrible burning in his heart and he fought to keep conscious.

'But everything changes and it's time for a new era.'

Spinks saw Adam was wearing a pair of Mrs Mitchell's slippers. Very clever. He'd not be leaving noticeable fibres and tracks for the forensics team.

'Think about all the rumours and whispers after your death. Why did he come here alone? Why didn't he call for support? And what about when they find out about Jennifer? Then the fireworks will really fly.'

Adam leaned into Spinks' face. 'Oh yes, I know about that, old man. And soon everyone else will know too because I'm going to make sure of it.'

Mitchell laughed again. A mad person's laugh, and a victor's laugh.

Chapter Fifty

10.38pm. Clarence House lay dark and silent. Marty tiptoed towards Beatrice's office.

Could she find the identity of the woman in Arizona? Might there be a clue in the personnel files? Was Beatrice implicated and then been clever enough to hide her involvement?

All Marty could hear was the hammering of her own heart. Softly closing the door to the manager's office, Marty flipped the lamp switch. A warm pool of light spilled onto the desk.

The bottom drawer of the filing cabinet gave a squeal of metal against metal. She quickly pulled out the fat pad of Beatrice's details and began skimming until she found the curriculum vitae. Beatrice had worked for not-for-profit organisations, all based in London, for the last fifteen years. There were references from Beatrice's former employers, which backed up the employment record. If this was to be believed, it placed Beatrice outside the net of suspects for the Arizona case.

As she slumped back in the chair, another thought occurred to Marty. Clarence House wasn't off the hook yet, what about Miss Pringle? Like Kal said, no one was innocent until proven innocent.

It took a few short moments to locate Miss Pringle's file, but the folder was empty. Shit. If that wasn't suspicious, then what the hell was? Sweat began forming at Marty's temples. She must get to the counselling suite and search it.

The entrance was eerily quiet. The photographs which seemed so cheery in the day now appeared dark and menacing. Even the yucca plant threw out strange shadows. As Marty tiptoed past the residents' lounge, she felt a sudden draught against the perspiration on her skin. Her eyes swivelled to the front door and her heart jumped. It was on the latch. Surely she'd closed it? There was no way it had come open on its own.

The sounds of the building suddenly became magnified – the hum of a television on standby, the *click* of a radiator as it heated. Marty held herself still and strained to hear any trace of human noise. After three slow clicks of the radiator, she moved to the wall and pressed her back against the hard surface.

10.51pm. She had no time to be cautious, she must get on with it.

The dim emergency lighting along the corridor accentuated the shadows. Keeping her shoulder pressed against the wall, Marty inched forward. All her senses were jangling and her emotions kept spiking to the skies. Getting to the counsellor's door put more strain on her system than running a marathon. I'm going to find the evidence, I will not let Jennifer die, she thought grimly – Chloe Carter's torturer and any other sick shits have taken on the wrong person.

She was in full combat mode and ready for it, but no one jumped her. Marty slipped inside the counsellor's office and allowed herself a small breath of relief. Maybe she'd made a mistake with the entrance and not pulled it properly closed. No, she told herself, someone else is in the building and you've got to get what you want before they find you.

The drawers were full of the usual rubbish people filled their desks with. Marty rifled through, now not giving a damn and tossing items onto the floor. Someone was coming for her, she knew it. She must find that one gold nugget and she was damned if she was going to give up until she had it.

A slight noise outside told Marty she was out of time. Damn it, there was nothing here except junk. She flung a bundle of notes onto the floor and jumped up, sending the desk chair clattering. It was then she caught sight of a photograph sitting on top of the filing cabinet. Marty's blood ran cold.

The door flew open.

'What the hell-!' Miss Pringle stood with her hands on her hips.

Marty opened her mouth and nothing came out. In the photograph Miss Pringle was at the rim of the Grand Canyon, Arizona. Her hair blew in the wind and she was arm in arm with Alfredo Manson.

Chapter Fifty-one

'Oh course! Well done, Simon. Where else could you pick up something so nice for so little?'

Simon had called Kal with his findings. He'd discovered photographs of Ruth and Dougie in a high street. Dougie was standing outside a hospice charity shop and the window behind him was full of jewellery. Then there was a shot of the dragonfly brooch pinned onto Dougie's top.

10.38pm. Kal called Spinks direct to tell him to meet her at the charity shop. He didn't answer. What the hell was wrong with him? This was their final chance and the break they needed.

When a woman on Spinks' team told Kal he'd dropped off the grid, Kal felt sick to her stomach. So near to their deadline? Spinks would never do that.

The detective constable said a man claiming to be Adam Mitchell had called and Spinks left the office without explanation. Kal paced up and down the pavement. She glared at a passer-by who was unfortunate enough to give her a curious look, and the man scuttled off. Shit, what if it *was* Mitchell who phoned? And what if Spinks had taken the gamble of a rendezvous?

Only one thing would lure Spinks to take that risk. Mitchell must have made an offer or a threat. There would have to have been bait that was highly persuasive – which at this point meant life or death. As for a meeting point, Kal only had time for one, educated guess. She took off at speed.

It was breaking all her own rules to go after Spinks before Jennifer. Kal didn't need him for the raid on the charity shop, she didn't need him for stealth and she didn't need him for force. She didn't need him for anything. Yet she knew it was a lie. This investigation had shown her how much she did need him – she needed Spinks because he kept alive her belief in good men. Good men who'd give all they'd got to confront evil. It was the only thing which helped dilute her own experience with David Khan, who'd deceived her and turned out to be evil incarnate.

Twenty minutes maximum, that's all she could afford. After that, he was on his own.

***

The front door of Mrs Mitchell's house lay open. That was sign enough her guess had been the right one. The dusty, show-room lounge lay abandoned. Kal quickly searched the ground floor and found nothing.

The horrible smell struck Kal as soon as she headed up the stairs. She trod carefully, breathing lightly, her skin prickling.

By the time she got to the top, the hairs on the back of Kal's neck were standing on end. All her senses were heightened and she felt certain she could smell the tang of fresh blood.

She let her unconscious pick which room to enter first. Inside, she found all the horrors. Mrs Mitchell was dead, submerged in what appeared to be a bath of water and blood.

Spinks was on his back with the handle of a knife sticking out of his belly. He lay in a horrible dark pool. She moved quickly to his side.

'You old fool! I'd have come with you, no questions asked, you knew that didn't you? Why didn't you call me?'

Spinks was barely conscious.

'We can't fight crime if we don't work together. You're the one who taught me that, don't you remember?'

No blood was coming from between her fingers as she applied force to the wound. It was a bad sign.

In those few seconds, she let herself realise how much he'd come to mean to her.

'Hold on,' she said. 'The ambulance is on its way.'

Spinks' lips were moving and Kal bent close to listen.

While she waited for the sirens, Kal counted the minutes. 11.04pm. She could still make it.

She didn't leave Spinks until one of the ambulance crew was at his side. By then, he was chalk-white as a corpse though his heart still fluttered. She told herself he could pull through.

It took all her will power to push him from her mind and concentrate on the task ahead. Kal kicked into emergency mode, full of adrenalin and rage. She must get to the hospice charity shop, and god help anyone who got in her way, for Jennifer and for Spinks.

Chapter Fifty-two

All the shops in the row had long since closed for the night and the street lay quiet. Somewhere in the distance a dog barked and a man's voice shouted out, telling it to shut up.

A street lamp played on the charity shop window. The corner of the display was still full of jewellery, including a few antique items, and light sparkled on the gemstones. Kal gritted her teeth – to a homeless young woman and her vulnerable friend, they had glittered like diamonds.

The shop had three floors above and everything appeared plain and unremarkable. Two doors down was an estate agents and further on there were a couple of clothing shops. This was not the sort of place where you'd expect women to be incarcerated, or invited for auditions which turned into violent encounters and rape. Yet she knew this was the right place. Kal could feel it in her bones.

11.32pm. She must expect Adam and his brother to be here, and there might be others. As usual, she carried no weapons. She had kung fu and Dim-mak, and she had the greatest weapon of all according to her father, and she agreed – which was a cunning mind.

The first challenge was to find a stealthy way of entering. No windows were open at the front of the house, nor any amongst the neighbouring properties in the terrace. Around the back, it was a different story. A second-floor window had been cracked open for ventilation.

All the information they'd got pointed to the likelihood of a final sacrifice tonight. Why would the perpetrators be careless enough to leave a window open? Wouldn't they be worried about what Ruth could tell? The clever minds at work here must feel utterly secure, the bastards – they weren't expecting anyone on their trail. Either that, or they *were* expecting a caller and they'd left a little invite. A little bit of cheese in the trap. Kal's skin flashed hot and cold. Either way, she was going in.

She scaled the building, using the neighbour's balcony and then the drainpipe. For the last stretch she inched her way along, clinging to the gaps between the bricks with her fingers, a spine-crushing fall yawning beneath her.

Reaching the window, Kal eased it open. No window lock had been engaged. 11.47pm. She rolled inside.

She landed with a soft *plop* onto the carpet. The house lay in darkness and she let her pulse settle as she lay still as stone. Apart from the window she'd just opened, no light filtered from outside because all the windows were blacked out. It meant she'd be moving in the pitch dark. Shit. But she knew she could do it. David Khan had taught her how.

She rolled to her knees and checked the room layout before closing the window back down to a crack. Then she trailed her fingertips lightly along the wall, walking towards the door on the other side, feeling with her foot for each step.

Out in the hallway it was pitch black and she could not be one-hundred per cent sure she was alone. Was someone observing her in the dark? It was possible. Yet she must force herself onwards and keep alert. Locating the women was her priority.

***

The new Grand Master congratulated herself. Getting rid of her predecessor had gone to plan, even down to goading them into stabbing the detective. Stephanie felt that final act of defiance and a final murder was a fitting end for her mother.

Tonight would be Stephanie's inauguration and she would give new life to The Lodge with a final Ceremony. Caressing the mother of pearl handle, she laid the knife in its special place. They would use the old methods on the blonde detective. She looked forward to hearing her scream.

After tonight's entertainment, they would jet off for a new start in Detroit. And yet, there was a fly in the ointment. A human fly that was right this moment scaling the outside of the building. Stephanie hadn't believed for a moment there was anyone on to them. She'd ordered Adam to leave the window open simply because caution was her second nature, in case Spinks had alerted a colleague, which she severely doubted was possible. Who would have the audacity to come here, alone?

Stephanie bit back her outrage. How dare someone spoil her evening. Who was this human nuisance? Whoever this fucker was, they were adept at clandestine entry and they certainly had some balls. It looked like she had a smart one to deal with. Now that could be fun.

***

Back at Clarence House, Marty made a split-second decision. Miss Pringle wasn't alone, Adam Mitchell was by her side and Marty allowed herself to be captured. She could have fought them off but with time running out she'd wanted them to lead her to Jennifer.

'You fucking animals.' Marty spat in Adam Mitchell's face as he bound her hands.

'Gag her,' Miss Pringle said. 'I don't want to listen to that bitch's shit.'

A short drive and she was bundled out of the back of a van and frog-marched along a quiet row of shops. Marty had to be careful not to choke because they'd rammed a rag into her mouth before covering it with tape. The rag threatened to go down her windpipe at any moment.

Inside the house, Marty got her wish – they brought her to the other women. Oh fuck, thought Marty, they're not only deviant, these two are completely insane. One woman lay in a heap on the floor of her cell. Half her skin was missing. Marty feared she was dead, though when she looked closely she thought she saw the woman's chest moving. Or was it her imagination?

Jennifer was in a second cell. The police woman lay on the floor clutching the bars and she was trying to speak, though it seemed she had trouble breathing.

Miss Pringle was in control and she ordered Jennifer to be brought with them upstairs to the top of the house.

***

When Jennifer heard people coming, she roused herself ready to plead for Kirsten's life. For a moment she was confused because they weren't wearing masks or robes. They were real people.

'Please...' she said. They ignored her. They were dragging a black woman behind them. She could see the black woman's eyes were full of anger.

'Please. Help her,' Jennifer said.

The woman in charge laughed and licked the side of Jennifer's face with her tongue.

'I know you like it,' Stephanie said. 'And you're going to like what comes next even more. You're coming with me.'

The woman pressed her mouth onto Jennifer's and then they were taking her.

'No,' she said. 'No, I won't leave her.'

Out the corner of her eye, Jennifer tried to catch a last glimpse of Kirsten as she was dragged away.

***

Marty stared at Stephanie with hatred.

'Tell me who the fuck that is outside the house,' Stephanie shrieked.

My god, the woman was losing it, Marty thought. She hoped Stephanie would throw herself on the floor and kick and scream and that it would buy Kal more time. Because that figure had to be Kal.

Stephanie ripped the tape from Marty's face, pulling skin away with it. Marty blinked away tears of pain.

'Who the fuck is it!'

Stephanie made a leap for the ceremonial knife and held it at Marty's neck.

'Tell me or I'll cut you limb from limb.'

'Do it then. You're no match for my friend.'

That earned her a slash and now blood flowed onto Marty's chest. It wasn't life threatening, she thought, as Adam re-gagged her, ramming the rag even further down her throat than before.

'Get the goggles on,' Stephanie ordered. 'And whoever it is, deal with them.'

Marty watched as Stephanie settled behind the screen of a laptop and connected up the feed from Adam's infra-red goggles.

***

There was a light switch in the hallway which didn't function. Then there were several doorways. Kal tested them all like a blind person, running her hands down each frame to find the handles. They were all locked and as Kal continued, she started to get a strange feeling. It was a nasty, cold, creepy feeling with an edge of fear. The same feeling she used to get when her father stalked her. The further she went, the more the feeling grew, until her own mind started whispering the word "Trap".

Kal used her discipline to keep moving. If this was a trap, what choice did she have except to continue and find how it played out? She must learn where her opportunities lay. And discover where her opponents were weak.

The dark made her vulnerable though not as vulnerable as they'd assume. They wouldn't know David Khan had made a habit of stalking her in the dark and made her do the same to him. No, the cards are pretty evenly stacked at this point.

A lighter current of air told her she'd reached the end of the hallway. If they wanted to kill her they could have. A bullet would do the trick, or the stab of a knife from a doorway, and they hadn't done it. Which meant this was a game. Kal imagined her own father whispering in her ear, telling her what to do. At the end of the hallway she faced a choice – up or down. She chose down.

Her back flashed hot then cold and prickles of electricity kept running up and down her arms. It was the adrenalin going into overdrive because the more she continued the more her instincts told her she was being watched. Eyes were on her. In her estimation, someone was creeping up behind. How close were they? If they attacked on the stairs, they'd have the advantage of height, which she didn't at all like the idea of. So she moved a little more quickly, feeling for each step, wary of tripwires. Wary of electric shocks. Wary of booby traps.

***

Adam adjusted his infra-red goggles. He'd watched from the end of the hallway as the intruder exited the first room. And he'd been surprised because he'd expected it to be a man. His night-vision goggles picked her out in red, showing her heat outline and the hot spots of her body. The woman was groping her way forwards in the pitch black. Adam bit back a snigger at how ridiculous she looked, and how helpless.

Upstairs in the throne room, the new Grand Master would be watching the live feed and Adam wondered if she'd be wetting herself with anticipation.

Adam was getting excited. Whoever she was, she was scared and she'd speeded up. He wanted to reach out a hand and touch her hair, my God he was so close he could almost do it. He crept along behind her,

273

matching his footsteps to hers so he made no sound, and with each footstep he closed the distance between them.

***

On the next level down, Kal felt another change in the air. And she got a waft of decay and fear and human rot that almost made her gag. She steadied herself and kept her back to the wall. As soon as the person following her made a mistake, she'd take him. For now, it was time to play along and pretend she had no idea he was there. And time to take a risk. In games like this, the winner takes it all.

'Is anyone there?' she called out.

There was movement up ahead. It was a scuffling like an animal. Kal's heart started going double time. Venturing into what felt like an open space ahead of her was high risk. What if there really was a wild animal here? Maybe chained up? No, she didn't think so, that was only fear speaking. There were no monsters here, only human beings. And the women she was searching for.

Kal crouched low, making her way towards the noise. It didn't take many steps before she came up against metal bars. She felt them up and down – these were the bars of a cell.

'Is someone there?'

Again, there was a shuffling and she caught the sound of rapid breathing from the other side. Then something hot and slippery flopped onto her hand. Kal had to stifle a scream before she realised it was another hand. A human one. Oh god.

Kal grasped the hand with both of hers.

'Who are you? she said. 'I'm here to get you out.'

Why was the hand so hot and limp and sweaty?

Now she felt breath on her face and it was the hot breath of a sick person. A woman's voice whispered something, and Kal bent close to hear. 'Wom-'

The danger signals from behind had been ramping up. They were getting closer and closer. Kal held herself very still, sensing her moment to strike. She wanted to attack – she wanted to leap and maim and find the fucking lights and get this woman out. She squeezed the hand and then dropped it. Her muscles felt like coiled steel as she prepared to spring.

'It's going to be okay.'

Adam knew the guest couldn't speak because he'd put tape over her mouth. He pushed his arm forward, ready to press the stun gun into the intruder's back. He couldn't wait to see her jerk and spasm. Very likely she'd piss herself. This was going to be great.

At that moment, Kal suddenly pushed away from the bars. As he jerked back in surprise, the brush of Adam's clothing made a tiny noise. It allowed her to better judge the distance and the direction of her pursuer and adjust the trajectory of her attack.

Kal brought them both to the ground. Adam tried to jab the stun weapon into her face but his goggles had been knocked askew and he couldn't see properly. Kal had an iron grip on his wrist and she overpowered him in a matter of seconds, forcing her thumbs down onto his pressure points. Yet she didn't want him unconscious because she needed answers. Ripping the goggles away, she wrapped the strap around his neck and twisted.

'How many of you in the house?'

Adam let out a gargle and she twisted the strap tighter.

'I said, how many?'

'Four.'

'Tell me the truth fucker, or I'm going to kill you.'

'Two.'

She wanted to smash his head into the floor until he was senseless. Wanted to enact such violence on him he'd never walk again, maybe never speak again. He'd raped, he'd tortured, he'd taken lives. Kal saw red.

'Where's Jennifer?'

'You're too late,' he said. 'She's already dead.'

Answering with defiance was probably the biggest mistake of Adam Mitchell's life. Kal brought his head up and then slammed it into the floor. There was a horrible crunch. She wondered if she'd fractured his skull. Adam went limp, though he was still breathing. That was a shame, she thought, she should have used more force.

'You're lucky I don't kill you on the spot, you fucking piece of shit,' she said, to his motionless body.

Using his equipment, Kal could now see the slumped figure in the cell. From the high heat readings, the woman had a fever.

'I'm coming back for you. But first I'm bringing down the sick shit behind this hell-hole. And that isn't you, is it Adam.'

***

Marty's wrists were bleeding freely where she'd been working against the restraints. All she needed to do, Marty thought darkly, was rip the skin off her own wrists, like peeling a grape, and then she might be able to slip one hand through. Marty felt she was very close and she'd damn well keep trying. The other problem was the rag, which kept threatening to slip further down her throat.

Immobilised on a stone slab, Jennifer's arms were pinned at right angles to her sides. They'd drugged her and her eyeballs kept rolling into the back of her head. The knife that would be used for cutting Jennifer's wrists had been placed on a stone tablet. Marty had cringed to see how they'd handled the knife so carefully, as if it were a precious item rather than a butcher's instrument. She'd locked eyes with Jennifer for one precious moment.

The two perps talked and laughed together like demons. And they were going to sacrifice Jennifer. Then they'd probably kill Marty once they'd got their kicks out of making her watch. Desperation and anger mixed together as Marty continued her efforts behind her back.

'Never send idiots to do real work,' the new Grand Master muttered to herself.

Stephanie had watched how easily the intruder overcame Adam. Then again, her younger brothers had always been useless shits who lacked real stuffing. That's why their mother had been able to dominate them. And why Stephanie planned to do the same.

The Grand Master watched as Kal searched the house and a brilliant idea popped into her mind.

What about a little surprise for their new visitor? Why not take the game up to the next level and see what this intruder was made of?

'Shall we have a real party?' said the Grand Master. 'I think it would be a fitting finale to our London activities, don't you? Oh come on now you black bitch, haven't you got anything to say?'

The arrival of Kal had interrupted the ceremonial preparations. Marty couldn't see the laptop screen from her position on the floor, though Stephanie had given Marty a gloating, running commentary, right up to a string of obscenities and expletives when Kal took Adam down.

Knowing her friend had crossed that hurdle, Marty felt a surge of renewed hope.

Miss Pringle, who Marty now knew was Stephanie Mitchell, started packing away her computer. Then she disappeared out of the room and Marty strained to reach the ceremonial knife with her foot. It was tantalisingly out of reach. When Stephanie Mitchell came back, Marty stared. Stephanie was covered in blood from head to foot. The woman had even smeared it into her own hair so globules dripped from the ends. Marty stared in revulsion.

Then Stephanie Mitchell sat against a pillar, mimicking Marty's position. She put her hands behind her back and slumped to the side.

Fuck! The evil shit was setting a trap. Marty went ballistic, thrashing against the ties, until she almost suffocated as the rag slipped down her throat. For a moment, she feared she'd vomit and then choke on the result.

***

Kal had finished checking the first floor. Now she headed to the top of the house and saw one room ahead with dim lighting. She prepared mentally for the encounter. This was it. This was what she'd come for.

As she entered, she flung aside the goggles, scanning the room quickly. The breath caught in her throat. One woman lay on a slab, battered and naked, spread-eagled, her arms exposed ready for cutting. Marty was tied to a pillar with blood covering her chest and she was thrashing and trying to grunt beneath a gag. And a third woman, terribly injured and with blood pouring down, was propped up over the other side of the room. The effect of three victims at once, one of them her best friend, was almost overwhelming.

And where was the chief perpetrator? The one who pulled all the strings? Were they hiding close by or had they already escaped? She must find them before they got away scott-free and set up elsewhere. The sick master mind wouldn't get away with it like they did in Arizona, oh no, not on her watch. She must be quick.

Kal ran to the woman with the severest wounds. The seconds were ticking but she must check and stabilise the victims before she could go after the monster.

It was as she knelt, Kal had a sudden instinct to pull back.

Part of the impulse was a question which had dogged her since she discovered Spinks. How could he have been overcome, seemingly so easily? Whose hand held the knife? She'd seen the angle of the blade – as if Spinks, tall as he was, had been leaning over at the time of the strike. For instance, leaning over the tub. Which would mean Mrs Mitchell was a killer. Part of the impulse was due to Marty's thrashing. Marty wanted to say something urgent, Kal felt sure of it, yet she'd no time to find out what. All along, Kal had felt it was too easy to get inside the house. Almost as if someone had wanted her here. And what had the woman downstairs been trying to say? Had a mastermind lured her in and was now ready to spring the trap?

Kal pulled back.

It wasn't completely in time and Stephanie Mitchell lunged with the stun gun. It got Kal. A jolt of pain shot up Kal's leg and she buckled, her muscles on that side going into spasm. She saw Stephanie pulling back for a second strike, her eyes white and crazy amongst the blood-red. Kal rolled out of reach and Stephanie shrieked and threw herself after Kal.

Desperation forced Marty to endure the final agony and twist one wrist free. With her free arm, she reached to full stretch and grabbed the sacrificial knife. Kal would only have one chance. Without hesitation, Marty threw it in a high arc to her friend.

Screaming obscenities, the woman on top of Kal seemed to have lost her mind. Kal was sufficiently incapacited she struggled to gain a proper grip and she received a second zap to her torso. Kal saw stars. It was then that the woman on the sacrificial table roused herself. She seemed to come to her senses for a few seconds and she croaked out one word. Knife. Kal understood and she turned her head to see the flash of an object spinning through the air.

Stephanie had a look of triumph on her face as she anticipated her final strike, and Kal shot out a hand to grab the sacrificial knife as it skittered across the floor. Then she plunged it upwards into her opponent's hand, almost slicing it in two.

The woman screamed and blood and spit rained on Kal's face. Kal rolled over and pinned down her opponent.

'You bitch! You fucking bitch!' The woman screamed.

Kal had to slap her around the face to stop her shrieking.

'I'll cut you up one slow piece at a time! You fucking bitch.'

'That'll be difficult when you're locked in an institution for the criminally insane.'

'How dare you speak to me like that! On your knees!'

Kal shot her friend a look. Marty was untying herself.

'Stephanie Mitchell is barking mad, in case you didn't notice.' Marty said.

'I'll rip the skin off your body you bastard! I am the Grand Master.'

'I don't think you are,' Kal said. 'Wasn't your mother the Grand Master and now she's dead.'

'I killed her and it's all mine.'

'You're sounding like a moron,' Kal said. 'Come over here Marty will you, and gag this one for me? Before I have to crack her skull like I did with her brother.'

Chapter Fifty-three

It didn't take long to locate Dougie. Kal found him in the corner of a room upstairs. When she set him free, Dougie wrapped his arms tightly around Kal. Thank goodness he had no physical injuries.

Jennifer and Marty were taken straight to hospital and Kal returned downstairs where specialised equipment had been called in to cut the woman out of her cell. Despite an extensive search of the property, they'd not been able to find the key anywhere. Kal insisted on staying with the victim until she was freed. She sat scrunched against the bars behind a protective shield and holding the woman's limp hand. Sparks flew as the fire service sliced through metal.

Despite the grime and the emaciation and the terrible burning of her body, Kal recognised this victim. It was Ivana Stanislova. She stroked Ivana's blonde and matted hair.

The ambulance crew had already set up a drip and monitoring system for Ivana. She was slowly fading, but the crew were confident they'd be able to stabilise her. Kal whispered in Ivana's ear and continued to talk even when the girl's eyes were closed. She couldn't remember exactly what she said, though she had a feeling she drifted to telling about Spinks and how he'd risked everything to find them.

Once Ivana was in the ambulance, Kal planned to fetch Mrs Stanislova. She'd take her straight to the hospital to be reunited with her daughter. Kal was only sorry Spinks wouldn't be there to see it.

Downstairs in the basement, police located the freezer and the bodies of Tom Mitchell and Samson.

As for the surviving Mitchells, Adam was tight-lipped, whereas Stephanie was the opposite. She was livid and raving. Once her gag was removed, she shrieked at the police officers holding her down. Stephanie ranted about The Lodge being hers and how it was her inheritance and how dare they touch her. It seemed, after killing off her own mother, this was supposed to be her moment of glory.

'Like mother like daughter,' one of the police officers said, as Stephanie was taken into custody. 'What a bloody madhouse.'

Chapter Fifty-four

'A mother finally at peace,' Spinks said. He sighed, gazing at the screen of Kal's phone. 'Thank you for bringing this. It's these moments which make all the sleepless nights and the strain worthwhile. It reminds me why I became a detective in the first place.'

Kal helped herself to some of Spinks' grapes.

'Mrs Stanislova and Ivana made me video their message several times until they got it how they wanted it,' Kal said. 'Mrs Stanislova was sorry you haven't been able to visit them but given you've been in intensive care that would have been difficult. The reunion was wonderful. You'd have loved it.'

He smiled and shifted a little further up the pillows. Then he watched their message of thanks once again.

Over the last couple of days, Spinks had been directing the closing down of the operation from his hospital bed. He'd insisted on it, despite objections from the doctors.

In keeping with her deranged ranting at the time of her arrest, Stephanie Mitchell confessed her part in the Arizona crimes, or, more accurately, vaunted her exploits. They had plenty to keep her imprisoned for the rest of her life. Chloe Carter could finally live in peace.

'The man connected to the new satellite in Detroit is under surveillance and he probably will be for the rest of his life,' Spinks said. 'We were able to locate him quickly thanks to Stephanie Mitchell's laptop. All the loops have been closed. I'm certain nothing has been missed this time. Thanks to you.'

Kal shrugged. 'No problem.'

'And I'm sure you'll be pleased to hear Ian Taylor has been suspended from duty pending a psychological evaluation. Via Samson, the Mitchell crew had been manipulating Taylor for years.'

It was a relief to hear he was off the streets. She stuffed her mouth with a few more grapes. 'You should have called me for the meeting with Adam. We all need someone to watch our backs.'

'I made a mistake.'

'Hey, we're all human.' She cleared her throat. 'Er, and I hear Jennifer plans to be back as soon as she's got a clean bill of health?'

'That won't be for a couple of months at least.'

Kal could hear the protectiveness in his voice and Spinks was giving her a strange look. She thought back to the moment in Mrs Mitchell's bathroom and the few words he'd whispered. She'd wondered long and hard about keeping quiet about that, except of all people, she knew how poisonous secrets could be, and how damaging.

Spinks trained as a junior police officer in Brighton and it didn't take a genius to work out the link between him and Jennifer. Kal was pretty certain she now knew why Mrs Stanislova had such an effect on Spinks. And she knew why he'd spent the entire investigation messing with the eagle pin at his lapel, and who had given it to him.

Spinks handed Kal back her phone and she met his eye. Spinks gave a sad smile. 'She died of cancer.'

Kal didn't know what to say.

'It's all right, I know you've guessed the truth. Jennifer is my daughter. I was a young recruit and Jennifer's mother was a senior social worker on the Brighton team. That's why I didn't want you to go there. Her name was Alice.'

The same name he'd whispered in the bathroom. *'Tell Alice I'm sorry.'*

'I'd have been happy to accept paternity and take my responsibilities. Alice didn't want it. I was ten years her junior and she was a high-flying professional. It was only a fling as far as she was concerned. She and her husband raised Jennifer and Alice told me to keep out. When Alice was diagnosed with cancer, she got back in touch. I was astonished Jennifer had become a London detective. Alice made me keep my promise never to tell Jennifer I was her father.'

'And you kept that promise.'

'As soon as I had a chance I took Jennifer onto my team. I simply had to be close to her and there wasn't a day went past I wasn't tempted to blurt it out. As you know I've my own adult children and Jennifer reminded me so much of Alice. She's such a talented young woman. Maybe one day I'll just tell her.'

'It must have been terrible when she went missing. That's why you called me in, wasn't it?'

Spinks seemed tearful. 'I'd been so busy thinking about her career and she'd practically begged me for the assignment. She was a perfect fit. I called you in because you were my best bet at finding her.'

Kal put her hand over his. 'Hang on a moment no, *we* were the best bet at finding her.'

And that's when Kal decided to tell Spinks her own secrets about her father. The ones only Marty knew, about David Khan's life of deceit as a vile criminal. Spinks wasn't surprised, maybe he'd guessed half of it. When she finished the shameful account, she made a request she'd wanted to make for a long time. She asked Spinks to help her find the child that lived – the child she'd found out about when she was searching for her mother, the child who survived her father's final killing assignment. She was going to make that right, whatever it took.

Chapter Fifty-five

Marty hadn't seen Kal like this in a long time, or maybe, she'd never seen her so happy. Part of the shadow which followed her friend around had disappeared. As Marty's mother would say, Hallelujah.

They'd all been invited to Dougie's birthday party. Ruth and Jennifer were over by the long table, arranging the food platters, and Simon was lighting the candles on the cake.

'I'll be having myself a big slice of that, it looks delicious,' Marty said to Kal.

Kal smiled. 'I had some more good news this morning. My homeless friend, Tilly, has got a part-time job at the cat rescue. Know anyone who wants a cat?'

'How about LeeMing, he could probably be persuaded.'

'You're kidding me, right?'

'Yeah, I am. I'd fear for the safety of any animal left in his care.'

'Now that's unfair,' Kal said with a laugh.

Dougie blew the candles out and they all sang for him and watched as Dougie cut the cake. Ruth picked up her guitar and started playing in the background. It took a few moments for Kal to realise Ruth was strumming her favourite song, Balm in Gilead, the one

Kal had played for her at the hospital. Across the room, the two of them met each other's eyes.

Marty noticed the moment and she put her arm around Kal and pulled her close. 'Glad that's all over,' she said.

'Hmm.'

Spinks was over the other side of the room, helping hand around the cake. Mrs Stanislova had sent a photograph of Ivana surrounded by her family, and Kal knew Spinks kept a framed copy on his desktop.

'Here's to a quiet life for a while,' Marty said.

'Don't put your slippers on yet,' Kal said. 'I've got some ideas for our next project.'

Marty rolled her eyes. 'Oh good. Not.'

'Oh yeah, and it seems we're semi-official. I'll get to pick and choose, and we're an official resource for the Organised Crime team.'

'Maybe we won't have to worry about paying the bills after all.'

Kal clinked glasses with Marty.

'Cheers,' Kal said. 'And here's to an exciting year ahead.'

****

London Noir (Kal Medi book 2)

The greater the evil, the more deadly the game...
A predator who kills prostitutes
And they've started a new killing spree

Kal goes undercover to track a predator who kills prostitutes.
Quiet for years, the signature killer has started a new spree.

She befriends Sophie, a troubled young woman.
Sophie suffers from nightmares and memory loss.
Her prostitute mother was murdered when she was a child. Sophie was there and she can't remember a thing about it.

But the killer is moving closer, hiding in plain sight, realising it's time to kill the one who got away...

The creepiest killer you'll meet this year...
Grab your copy today.

Chapter One

Sophie dipped her brush in water and chose sky blue to finish the detail. The colour reminded her of summer days. It also reminded Sophie of her mother, and, as usual, that brought a bitter taste to the back of her mouth. Sophie swallowed. Concentrating to stop the trembling in her fingers, with two strokes, she finished the butterfly wings. The makeup brush clattered onto the dresser. Sophie twisted towards the mirror and admired the trail of tiny, blue butterflies sweeping over her shoulder.

Her clutch bag was on the bed and she placed inside it the syringe, loaded and ready for its victim. Then she picked up the perfume and pepper spray, the jasmine scent sickly sweet. The spray was a noxious mix, designed to blind the victim and, even better, make them writhe in agony. For that reason, Lady Penny insisted all the girls carried it.

Last, Sophie took the flick knife and touched her finger to the razor-sharp edge. Sugar G had trained them – a strike to the eye, to the crease of the groin, or the stomach – all the soft parts of the body. Not all the girls carried a knife, and she was certain of those who did, none of them carried it to commit murder.

Praise for *London Noir*

'A five-star thriller which keeps you guessing until the end' *Jules 1960*

'Highly recommended' *Ellie S*

'Had me hooked from the beginning' *SandyJ21*

'An absolutely fantastic read' *S.A.W.*

'Brilliant!' *Dash fan*

'...an absolute stunner of an ending. Highly recommended.' *Kaz Angel*

'Action-packed, suspenseful, and eerie...' *Zoe*

'A thoroughly good read that makes me wish book three was already available'

'The creepiest killer of 2017' *Bloomin' Brilliant Books*

Grab your copy today !

Good Girl Bad Girl (Kal Medi book 1)

The darkest crimes can't stay hidden forever

A **dead journalist?**
A **dead matron** of a children's home
A **young body** washed up by the river

And a crime so evil it defies belief

Good Girl Bad Girl is an ERIC HOFFER BOOK
AWARD FINALIST 2017 and a READERS'
FAVOURITE Five Star Book.

Prologue

Alesha could no longer feel her legs.

They hung, freezing and lifeless beneath the surface of the water. Tied above her head, Alesha's wrists rubbed raw against the restraints. No point in struggling. She tried that already, for hours or was it days? All the panic and the terror had long since run out of her and coursed down her legs.

And the pool deepened. When the water lapped her bellybutton, the flesh on Alesha's stomach contracted. Her two tormentors had climbed a ladder to escape, and a faint light drifted down from their exit route. Alesha watched the gleam of the rungs as they disappeared one by one beneath the inky blue.

How many times had she endured it? Twice, she thought, or was it three times? Each submersion, they stripped away her strength. Each time she was left with less of her self. They were paring her down layer by layer. Perhaps this time she'd be down to bare bones and the last shreds of will. Or perhaps this time she wouldn't make it.

Alesha shuddered as the water climbed her rib cage. Once it reached the level of her heart, she'd only have a few moments before she drowned. The dread rose up. She tried not to think about the moments ahead, pushing away the thought of them resuscitating her, then closing in for the interrogation, their violence and their voices filling every cell in her body.

Lapping at the sides of the chamber, the water sounded like gentle waves at the seaside. Alesha pressed her eyes closed. She wouldn't crack. She'd never tell them. They'd have to kill her first. The thought almost made her laugh. Yes, she'd wondered about that too, wondered if she were losing her mind. Thing is, if she were dead she wouldn't be able to give anything away. So perhaps she shouldn't fight it. Maybe it'd be better to take that one last breath as deep as she could and hope her heart gave out. Then the water would take away her secrets.

As the water rose, Alesha pushed deep inside her own mind and she saw her husband and he was young, like he'd been when they first met. He smiled at her. And the water reached her throat.

Now she could see her daughter, Kal, running with her black hair streaming out in the wind. At first, Kal was a little girl laughing, and then she was a fiery teenager, and then she became a young woman. Alesha took a deep breath and sealed her lips closed. Kal was shouting and determined and running towards Alesha. Alesha knew Kal'd never reach her in time. The water covered Alesha's nose and she felt the air expanding in her chest. Fight against it, she commanded herself. Don't take a breath. Her body thrashed and jerked. They'd turn the water off soon. Then they'd bring her back from the brink. Then they'd start again. Alesha felt a deep regret for handing her daughter a death sentence. Then she blacked out.

Praise for Good Girl Bad Girl

'A cracking read'
Amazon reviewer

'A taut, exciting thriller which had me hooked'
Reviewer, The Book Club TBC

"On the edge of my seat..."
Amazon reviewer

"A real kick-ass heroine and a great lead character..."
Grab This Book

"...A thriller that will keep you up at night."
The Serial Reader

'Dangerous territory for exploration in a first
novel...This is a terrific start for an author who
demonstrates strong promise. 5 stars."
Hall of Fame, Top 100 reviewer, Vine Voice

"An action packed thriller with a strong, independent
female character ... I look forward to reading the next in
the   series."
Reviewer, The Book Club TBC

"… multi-layered psychological thriller, I really enjoyed
Good Girl Bad Girl and look forward to reading the next
Kal Medi book."
BloominBrilliant Books

'Full of suspenseful twists and turns'
Amazon reviewer

Grab your copy today!

A note from Ann Girdharry

I hope you enjoyed *The Beauty Killers* and I'd like to say a huge thank you for choosing it.

This is the third instalment and Kal and Marty have other crimes to solve and challenges to face. I hope you enjoy reading about them as much as I like writing their stories.

Please leave a written review, for instance, on Amazon or Goodreads. They really make a difference and help others discover my books. Or maybe you can recommend *The Beauty Killers* to your friends and family…

If you'd like to keep up to date join my **Reader's Group**. I send everyone in my Reader's Group a note when I have a new release coming up and I'll let you know of any early 'read and review' opportunities.
(Don't worry, no spam, I promise.)

I usually offer a welcoming gift to new members. At the moment, it's my Chilling Tales of the Unexpected Boxed Set. You can find all the details on my webpage – www.girdharry.com

Happy Reading,
Ann Girdharry

Connect with me on social media –

follow my Facebook Author Page
https://www.facebook.com/AnnGirdharryAuthor/

follow on Goodreads
https://www.goodreads.com/author/show/14179591.Ann_Gir
dharry

follow on BookBub
www.bookbub.com/profile/ann-girdharry

My website *www.girdharry.com*

Acknowledgements

Beta readers are important because they are the very first reader's eyes on a book.

Alongside my editor, they're the ones who point out parts which are good and the bits that need more work, before I publish. A big thank you to Diane Miller, Mark B., Terje Iversen and VeggieReader for their insightful and generous comments.

Titles by Ann Girdharry

Kal Medi series

Good Girl Bad Girl
London Noir
The Beauty Killers

Chilling Tales of the Unexpected
Boxed Set

46047047R00186

Printed in Poland
by Amazon Fulfillment
Poland Sp. z o.o., Wrocław